OTHER BOOKS BY ROGER PINCKNEY

DEAD LOW WATER

DEAD LOW WATER

A NOVEL BY ROGER PINCKNEY

Little Rock, Arkansas
2019

www.RiversEdgeMedia.com
Published by River's Edge Media, LLC
6834 Cantrell Road, Ste. 172
Little Rock, AR 72207

Cover design by Paula Guajardo
Manufactured in the United States of America.
ISBN-13: 978-1-940595-68-9 softback
ISBN-13: 978-1-940595-69-6 ebook

DEAD LOW WATER

OUTSHINE THE SUN

February 5, 1958, in the skies high above Daufuskie Island, an Air Force B-47 was in trouble.

The bomber, under command of Major Howard Richardson, was on the way home to Homestead Air Force Base, Florida, after a simulated nuclear bombing of Radford, Virginia. Nobody really wanted to incinerate Radford except the Russians, for Radford was a major Cold War air defense radar site.

But no matter, in combat Richardson might have been flying out of Alaska to incinerate Vladivostok, homeport of the Soviet Pacific submarine and fishing fleets.

Until then, Radford would suffice.

The B-47 was carrying a four mega-ton hydrogen bomb.

Richardson thought the exercise was over when an F-86 Sabre Jet out of Charleston Air Force Base clipped his aircraft during a simulated gun-run. The impact sheared away number six engine, tore a gaping hole in the wing. The F-86 spun out of control but the pilot, Lt. Clarence Stewart, ejected and survived, though severely frostbitten from the high-altitude cold.

Lt. Stewart landed in the Savannah swamp, the South Carolina side. There were no gators awake in February to eat him as gators have done to survivors of aircraft crashes before. Stewart deployed his life raft and crawled inside, making a hasty shelter with his parachute. An hour later, came the chop-chop of a rescue helicopter. Stewart struggled with his flare pistol, but his frost-bitten fingers would not work. He nearly shot his own toes off and the flare exploded in his parachute tent. The chopper pilot never saw the fiery fiasco but the pop of the flare-gun set a hound to barking. The hound's owner tracked Stewart down, figuring him a deer poacher.

After doctoring his charge with moonshine, the rescuer attempted to call Charleston Air Force Base collect, but the charges were refused. Finally, in the hospital, the Air Force decided to amputate most, if not all of Stewart's fingers. When he threatened to go AWOL, they relented. Stewart eventually returned to duty and flew combat missions in Vietnam where he advanced to Wing Commander and earned a Silver Star, second only to the Congressional Medal of Honor.

Oddly, Stewart's F-86 did not crash, but landed, minus wings and pilot, but otherwise intact, in a cotton field outside Sylvania, Georgia.

But meanwhile, while Lt. Stewart was fretting over the gators, the stricken B-47 plummeted over three miles before Major Richardson regained control.

The crew requested permission to jettison the bomb to reduce weight and prevent the bomb from exploding during an emergency landing. Permission was granted, and the bomb was jettisoned at 7,200 feet while the bomber was limping along at 200 knots, barely airborne. The crew did not see an explosion when the bomb struck the sea. Richardson managed to land the B-47 safely at the nearest base, Hunter outside Savannah. Major Richardson and crew kissed the ground after getting safely upon it. Richardson was promoted to lieutenant colonel and awarded the Distinguished Flying Cross.

The 12-foot long Mark 15 bomb weighs 7,600 pounds and bears the serial number 47782. It contains 400 pounds of conventional high explosive and highly enriched uranium. Some sources describe the bomb as a fully functional nuclear weapon, but others describe it as disabled. If a nuclear detonation had occurred, or ever does occur, the possible blast effects would include a fireball with a radius of 1.2 miles, severe structural damage and thermal radiation causing third degree burns for ten times that distance.

A recovery effort began on February 6, 1958, for what is now known as the Tybee Bomb. The Air Force 2700th Explosive Ordnance Disposal Squadron and 100 Navy personnel equipped with hand held sonar and galvanic drag and cable sweeps mounted a search. On April 16, 1958, the military announced that the search efforts had been unsuccessful.

NARY A NOTHING

Daufuskie Island, forty-odd years later and a dozen miles away. The tide and the wind dropped off to nothing, a windowpane sea and nary a whisper from the beachgrass. Nary a rattle from the sweet green and yellow sea oats at his elbows, left and right.

Nary a nothing.

Crickets and copperheads held their breath, waiting on God's next move.

Hampy lay on his belly in the dunes, glassing the lowtide sandbars. Binoculars, cell phone and Glock automatic pistol. Camcorder, gnats, mosquitoes and horseflies.

Shit.

Hampy.

James Wade Hampton Waddell. Wade Hampton, the great Confederate general. Waddell, the intrepid rebel sea-raider. Time was he would rise up out of the tall grass and snatch a gun right out of a poacher's hands. And from there he steadily advanced towards likely assassination, deputized Federal now.

Deckhand on sport fishermen out of Oregon Inlet, illegal tuna sales to the Japs? Into the Great Smokies, scooting downhill though laurel thickets, busting hunters selling bear galls for Chinese quackery? Yep. Cockfights got right regular, upwards of a thousand roosters one year, all dead. Hampy nailed their asses and they never even saw it coming.

Hampy grew his hair out, dressed any which-away, drank on the job, chewed Bull of the Woods, smoked Camel straights and dope too, but only when necessary to maintain his cover.

He was one lucky cop.

But he was at the top of his pay, cheaper to retire than to plug his leaks. Lord knows what death benefits Eileen might get. Eileen. When he had her the first time, she broke a scent like sweet potatoes coming out the oven.

But he could not think about Eileen right now. He needed a bust and this wasn't it. Cops are not supposed to think that way but they do. You account for your time and the bean counters were always counting.

Hampy glassed the *Flying Cloud*, a pretty ninety-footer out of Thunderbolt Georgia, a wood boat, the last of her kind. Geechees built them on the creekbanks years gone by, cypress, pine and stalwart live oak. A flare at the bow and an arch astern, she had lines like a beautiful woman.

Easy duty watching a boat like that, excepting the bugs. But the birds were hanging in a great cloud just over the nets. The skipper was catching shrimp right where he was, no need to make a quick trawl up the creek.

You kept your ass out of the creek.

And the birds never lied.

Hampy was waiting on God's next move but God didn't move, so Hampy did. He glassed the boat one more time, elbowed his way down the backside of the dune.

He was a big man and he left a track just like a gator.

Daufuskie Island, two AM, late July.

Carla and Jeanie were sitting up with turtle nest number forty-two. Carla was five months pregnant with no man in sight. Two kids slept on a beach blanket ten yards away and called her momma. You could not see it there in the dark between the dunes, but I know them and can tell you. Carla had a splash of freckles across her nose and her eyes were green with splinters of pecan in each iris, drop dead pretty.

Jeanie was a pug-faced little blonde, tiny and very pretty too in her own way. She worked for the resort, managing the stables and taking tourists on beach rides. She took care of Carla's kids when she was not taking care of the horses.

Her boss would fire her if he caught her here. An endangered species on the beach was a great inconvenience, an impediment to commerce.

Jeanie drank when she was nervous and she smoked when she drank. Cruzan dark and crooked rum-soaked cheroots. The kids stirred and mumbled and they ran in their sleep like puppies, nosing the seawind, dog paddling their waters of dreams.

Loggerheads, three hundred pounds apiece, crawling ashore each summer to lay eggs in the dunes. Carla and the kids rode the beach each morning, May to October, following the cross-hatch herringbone tracks, locating and staking every nest. That was the easy part. Fifty-six days, when the dune sand cooled after sundown, a hundred or more hatchlings the size of poker chips boiled from each nest and made a rush to the sea. Coons, feral cats, fire ants, the odds were not good. The odyssey was no less hazardous than the trek. Only one in ten thousand, twenty-five years later, would come back to this very beach to lay.

But then there were the lights.

For three hundred million years, the hatchlings headed for the brightest thing they saw, star light and moon light on the restless waves. But now there were headlights, streetlights, condo lights. Night before, Carla fished two dozen hatchlings from the resort pool. She would not let that happen again.

They had a fine pissing match and she was still riled up. The resort manager, in his pleated khaki arrogance, claimed to be powerless in the matter. Carla printed out a copy of the county codes and lay it in his hand. He presented her with a photocopy of a page from his liability insurance, mandating a well -it pool area.

Quite frankly, he informed her on her way to the door, the fine was a lot less than potential liability exposure.

So, Carla stewed and steamed and called the turtle hotline and they promised to send somebody out. But meanwhile, get some documentation. Did she have a camcorder with infrared mode? She did not but Jeanie did.

"Mommy," one of the kids said sleepily, "I think I hear something."

"What does it sound like, Sweetheart?"

"Popcorn popping underground."

Carla reached for the camcorder. "Just don't get me on tape," Jeanie said.

"Ok," Carla said, "you run it."
She did.

Hampy's office was a pickup truck, four-wheel drive government green but no blue light, no radio, no government markings. Three-quarter ton, knobby tires with a regular commercial plate, registered to a fictitious name on a fictitious street in a fictitious trailer park in Cayce, South Carolina. But in back a carpenter's tool box was bolted and locked. Maps, flashlights, spotlights, handcuffs. Hand-held radio, GPS unit, camcorder, a digital camera with a long lens and a pump shotgun with a short barrel.

Hampy pulled off the highway, unlocked a gate, drove until the road became a track and then finally played out in a bog way down by the river. Headwaters of the Edisto, the longest blackwater stream in North America, water the color of strong ice tea, a tincture of leaves and rotting logs, lair of moccasins, alligators and swamp-ground haints.

Jesus, what a place! Rice fields hacked from hardwood swamp with the labor of slaves and indentured Irishmen, then a civil war and hurricanes turning it back to wild country again. Canals, forgotten islands, hummocks and bays, and always the great brooding cypress, the ruins of whiskey stills, the occasional pot plantation and marauding herds of man-eating boar. Bugs worse than anywhere this side of the Congo.

Vast stretches of this bottomland, here on the Edisto, and on the Combahee, the impassable swamps of the Ashepoo, the New River, and finally the Great Savannah and the Altamaha down in Georgia. God must have gotten careless when He drug His hand across this land. A man might see a timbered point a mile across the marsh but he might have to drive fifty miles to get to it.

Hampy drove to the shadow of a brush-line, wheeled the truck around to watch his backtrail. He did not figure anybody was following him, but then you never know. Hampy rattled around the cooler, came up with a brew.

It was mid-August and the wild black cherries were making fruit. A coon came out of the woods and shinnied up a tree. The coon came down the tree. Hampy popped his second brew. It was late afternoon and the deer ghosted the shade at the end of a clear-cut, waiting for dusk to venture into open ground. Way off to the east, an owl hooted for somebody who just died, or maybe for somebody just fixing to.

Hampy picked up this handheld. "Hampy calling Phantom, come in Phantom."

The radio popped and hissed.

"Hampy calling Phantom, what's your twenty?"

"Got you in my crosshairs, big boy," the radio said. "Don't make no sudden moves."

Phantom came by his name in high school, bogged down and drunk on the Hilton Head beach in his '56 Plymouth, a four-door with a big Hemi V-8 he called The Rock Crusher. You could drive on the beach back then.

"It's twenty bucks," the tow truck operator warned. "I pull you boys out and you don't pay, I make one call and you all go straight to jail."

"I'm Phantom Winchester III," he proclaimed, "and money is no problem!"

The tow truck extricated the Plymouth and when the boys emptied their pockets they had only seven dollars and small change.

They all went to jail and the name stuck.

Now Phantom was a sergeant, supervising enforcement across a dozen counties, from Georgetown to Georgia. His rise within the agency was a continuing source of astonishment among those who knew him best. He came up the most incorrigible poacher, trespasser and game thief and even as a junior officer indulged himself in considerable indiscretions.

He and Skeeter had a contest going, who could get the drop on who in the middle the night. In a more notable incident, Skeeter burglarized Phantom's house, crept down the hall and awoke him by softly cocking a loaded revolver in his ear. When Phantom attempted a counterattack, he found Skeeter's bed occupied by a woman who knew nothing of the contest. She was hauled to Emergency and sedated.

And then there was an incident on the Chesessee River, the officer allegedly drunk in the agency boat, tossing empties into the river, and shooting at them with his agency pistol. When an outraged citizen threatened to call the law, Phantom flashed his badge and grinned, "Lady, I *am* the law."

But like Hampy's wrestling matches, it was twenty years ago. "What you got for me?" he wanted to know. Phantom wore a perpetual grin and had the quick dark eyes of a weasel. He likely had his sights on Hampy, you could never tell.

"Not jack shit," Hampy said. "Shrimp are running offshore."

Phantom reached into his pocket and passed Hampy a square envelope. "Take a look at this CD when you get a chance. Some turtle team raising hell about resort lights. Been fishing hatchlings out of the pool. You got a beer?"

Hampy passed him one. "Ain't that an issue for county codes?"

"The light is Codes," Phantom said, "the turtles is we. Come up with one dead hatchling and it's a *taking*."

"Ten thousand bucks," Hampy whistled. "Want me to push that?"

"Hell no," Phantom grinned, "but feel free to scare the shit out of 'em. Stop at the courthouse and pick up somebody from Codes. And by the way, hang tight. We might need you."

"Something cooking?"

"Maybe. Got an APB on a couple from Hilton Head."

"Somebody we know?"

"Calverts, John and I forget the wife's name. They run the Harbour Town Marina. Live on a boat there. Nobody seen 'em in three days."

"Fish food?"

Phantom shrugged. "Dragging the boat basin tomorrow." Then he said almost as an afterthought. "They told me to give you a new phone."

Hampy changed phones like some men change socks. Some he bought at Walmart, used once, then either threw them overboard or crushed them beneath the tires of the truck. Chinese plastic ground to dust in the road or chaff on the tide, just a blip in cyberspace, no trace.

But you had to take care of the government phone. It was official and all conversations and texts were monitored and subject to subpoena.

A BUZZARD, GAPPING AND FLAPPING

Dragging. Three iron grapple hooks chained to six feet of iron pipe hauled behind an outboard. Back and forth, back and forth, real slow. You snag all sorts of stuff, anchors, junk outboard motors, boats, rope, plastic bags and clothes.

Sometimes clothes have corpses in them.

A body floats once it bloats, but meanwhile a shark could grab it, gone in a flash. A gator has no molars, so he sneaks meat, stashes it in a hole beneath the bank and gnaws daily while the body turns to brown cottage cheese. Crabs and little fish don't wait so long, eyes and lips first, then fingertips.

Only dental work and DNA for positive ID.

Gotta find that body quick.

Hampy wasn't thinking about bodies right then. Or at least not dead ones. Eileen was his wife of twenty-odd years and they had twin girl-children up and gone. She cut him to the bone the day they met and she cut him off the day he said he was going undercover. That lasted almost a month. Now he came home infrequently, and each time it was like a sailor coming home from the sea.

Hampy was back out of bed now, buck naked, a towel around his waist and the CD in his laptop. Back on the farm, everything he owned, his white clapboard house on his fifty-six acres on the end of a long dead-end road, debt free mostly. The driveway was rutted and pot-holed and Hampy would not fix it. Not much company in good weather and none at all in the rain. The window was open but only a fool would sit before a lighted window after dark. A Luna moth the size of a bat rattled against the screen. Frogs and crickets sawed away and down in the swamp another owl was asking questions way out in the dark.

Advance the video, run it backwards, look again. A woman and two half grown kids scrambling up and down the dunes in the quivering green of the infrared. Picking up something, yes, hatchlings headed the wrong way. Back and forth they went. Momma told them to be quick but to look where they stepped. The kids giggled and chattered. Another voice, the woman running the camera. Both of them pure old time Jasper County, country to the bone. Camera panned left and the screen went white from the lights around the pool. Digital imprint at the bottom of the screen. Four nights ago, 2:37 AM.

Good work, girls.

The woman was a looker, he could see that easy enough even in the tenuous flickering. Sharp nose, high cheekbones, pointy chin and wide-set oval eyes. Indian blood? Scandinavian? Something. Hampy loved girls and he got a shot of strange way back when, but like smoking dope, only in the line of duty.

But there was something else, another light over her shoulder. Hampy played it again and yet again. Yes, a boat out there that time of night, heading out the inlet at speed. Light from left to right, then it suddenly stopped and the light blinked twice. A puzzlement. Hampy copied the CD to his hard drive, popped it out, padded to the front hallway and set it on a table where he would not forget it in the morning.

The café was south of town between NAPA Auto Parts and the defunct Carolina Breeze drive-in theater, across the street from the sanctified hair salon where the flashing marquee read "Jesus is Coming Soon, Walk-ins Welcome."

The lot grew weeds and vandals stole all the speakers but the hurricane twisted remnants of the screen still stood, fluttering like some final flag of defeat. "Y'all got a lot of nookie here," it seemed to say, "but now you just stay home with the kids and watch TV."

Hampy got his share of nookie there, too, the first of it in his momma's car. He always threw the panties on the dashboard after he slipped them off his date. He was, of course, a gentleman, and did not want the lady's underpinnings loaded up with floorboard sand. Last thing before he went inside at the end of each evening, he made a quick swipe at any errant short and curlies with his hand. That worked well enough till first frost, when they piled into the car for church and Momma hit the defrost button and various shades of pubic hair took flight from the defroster vents and sifted down upon the family's Sunday finery.

No one said a damn thing, but the two miles to the church-house were the longest two miles of his life.

Now Hampy sat at a corner table, a world away but only two hundred yards from the scene of his first fornications. He ordered chicken fried steak, baked potato, house salad and a tap beer. He kept his back to the wall and his face to the door. The beer came up first. He drank it, ordered another. Hampy never drank odd numbers. One beer or three or five just didn't taste right. So it was always two, four, or a whole six pack.

He read a back issue of the *Savannah Morning News*, business section, page D-12, the shipping news. Savannah was a busy port, number three on the East Coast. Ships inbound that night, Oriental Princess, Hong Kong; Sea Star, Shanghai; Esso Energy, London; Ocean Rover, Monrovia; Island Trader, Colon.

Liberian or Panamanian didn't mean jack-shit. Those countries made an industry out of registering ships they never saw. Just sign the papers and attach an international bank draft. No unions, no inspections, no insurance, no questions. Greek owned, Ukrainian command, Indian engineers and Pakistani crew? Who knows what you might get? Korean, Taiwanese, Yemeni? Stinking and lousy rust-buckets et up with rats. The crews threw the rat boxes over the side, still full of poison and dead rats. Arsenic and the decaying flesh of the earth's vilest creature washed upon beaches hereabouts while the men swapped venereal diseases with the colored whores in the honky-tonks along US 80, up in Garden City, where the container ships unloaded spandex britches for bulging American women, cell phones and tennis shoes made with Chinese slave labor.

Hampy turned to the tide tables and tried to connect the dots. That boat leaving Harbour Town in the wee hours, then running square up on Grenadier Shoals. You can't leave Calibogue Sound and head straight to sea on dead low water. A local would have known that. The light flashing twice? Likely not a signal, but two people walking past three-sixty nav light to check the motors. So there were at least two people and there were outboards. At that speed there would have been at least two engines, maybe three. Hampy was damned proud of his police work, but from there on he was stumped.

So who in the hell was farting around out there anyway? What ship would they meet? Were they even going to meet a ship? Hampy pondered over the names, times, registrations.

Wasn't none of his business, no. Phantom was out dragging a boat basin and he was soon off chasing sea turtles. But Hampy was a cop and none of this rested easy on his mind. Maybe the turtle girls saw something the camera didn't catch.

Miss Ernestine brought out the order. She was a pretty brown girl, about the color of pecan pie. She was pushing forty and starting to spread, but she still looked mighty good. "Good morning, Mister Jim."

Hampy's given name was James. Down here, you have your father's name, your Christian name, your nick name. Otherwise, you are son-of-a-bitch or bastard. Hampy was a bastard to everybody he busted.

"Morning, Miss Ernestine." It was a few minutes past noon but that did not matter.

"Got dinner right here, Honey." She'd been crying, a husky rasp in the back of her throat and her fingers shook as she set the table. She tipped the beer and when she grabbed a napkin to keep the tsunami of foam out of his lap, his potato hit the floor with a dull thump, buttered side down. Ernestine threw her hands to her face and fled back to the kitchen.

Hampy turned to the barkeep. "What's ailing her?"

The barkeep shrugged. "Her uncle died last week."

Hampy cracked the kitchen door, peeped inside. Miss Ernestine had another potato going in the microwave and she stood at the prep table listlessly slicing carrots. "You okay, Miss Ernestine?"

"It's that buzzard, Mr. Jim."

"What buzzard?"

"Oh, Mr. Jim, he bust through the window glass an' come right in the porch!"

"Somebody die, Miss Ernestine?"

She nodded, daubed at her eyes with the back of her hand. "My uncle die. How you know that?"

"I just know that," Hampy said. He thought fast. "Listen here, Miss Ernestine, you didn't look him in the eye, did you?"

"No sir. He just lay there flapping and gapping."

"You didn't look him in the eye, you'll be okay."

"No sir, I never look him in the eye. I come back in two hour and he gone. Clean up the busted glass and burn the feathers in the stove." She glanced up from her work and her face froze in terror. Hampy followed her gaze to the window and beyond. A lone buzzard was roosting atop the defunct movie screen, looking squarely in their direction. Ernestine's knife clattered to the floor. She threw her hands to her face again. "Oh, Mr. Jim, I lie to you," she sobbed, "I look him square in the eye!"

She grabbed a towel and threw it over her head, like a man might do caught out in a hailstorm. She turned on her heel and ran shrieking through the back door. Hampy heard the roar of an engine, tires gathering gravel and finally the squall as they bit into the blacktop. His potato sizzled and shrank, abandoned and rotating on the microwave turntable. He buttered it himself and went back to his table, back to the wall, face to the door, as before.

THE BULGE IN KING HENRY'S BRITCHES

Deacon Limehouse sat on one side of the desk, Sheriff Nicky Jackitis on the other. Deacon Limehouse was an Episcopalian and the Episcopal Church did not normally have deacons. But he was leader of a splinter group, which met in private homes after the national church ordained an openly gay bishop. Deputies had broken down the door and interrupted a prayer service with drawn guns.

The Episcopal Church missed the Reformation, thanks to the bulge in King Henry's britches. That would be Henry XIII, a good long time ago, but not long enough. Henry wanted to get shut of Catherine of Aragon, his first of seven wives. She was a hottie, by most accounts. Though Henry screwed her joyously and incessantly, Catherine did not bear him a male heir to the throne. Henry did not know about the male Y chromosome and he figured it was Catherine's fault. Given what we know today about vaginal acidity and the survival of certain sperm, maybe Henry was right, even if he did not know why.

But the proposed dissolution was not taken lightly, as Catherine was sister to the king of Spain, and the two kingdoms had fought many wars. Pope Clement the Umpteenth, reckoning divorce proceedings would result in another bloodbath, denied Henry's petition.

King Henry was a pious man. Between erections he pondered and he prayed and came up with some obscure passage wherein Paul said God sent kings to rule over us for us for our own good. So, when God sorted it all out, anything a king would do was right. Right?

Suddenly enlightened, Henry proclaimed himself head of the English Church, seized cathedrals, churches, monasteries and considerable treasure in the process. He granted himself a divorce from Catherine, on the grounds the marriage had never been consummated. As this absurdity would have taken military action to reverse, it stood. And the average Episcopalian has been sucking Ecclesiastical Hind Tit ever since.

Sometimes it takes a long time for history to rise up and bite a man in the ass. Six hundred-odd years later, Deacon Limehouse got bit. Of all the Gifts of the Spirit, perhaps the greatest is the Light to see the Word as each man needs to see it. Luther said that, but the Episcopal Church did not truck with Martin Luther, and the deacon was under official censure and his ass was sore.

A philandering king to a queer bishop, Oh Sweet Suffering Christ! The deacon's congregation had been meeting in the same place since 1724. Heroes of the Revolution slept beneath dogwoods that bloomed each Easter like the wounds of Jesus. There was a plaque to the Civil War dead on the south wall, comprising fully one-third of the male congregants. Yankee bullet holes pocked the front door and slaves left their names carved upon the seats of the balcony, where Negroes sat in those olden days.

But none of this mattered. If you disagreed with the bishop, you were out.

The deacon's doctor prescribed anti-depressants which he refused, ant-acids which he did not.

But to the sheriff. Nicky Jackitis was the grandson of a Greek immigrant. Old Man Nikos Jackitis spoke broken English and fished sponges off Tarpon Springs until plastic ruined the natural sponge trade. The sheriff's father anglicized himself. Nick was a Marine, an MP who pulled duty at the recruit training base at Parris Island. Drill instructors and assorted support personnel, four or five beers into most any evening, took to speaking Vietnamese and beating on each other. Some mornings, Nick came home with blood on his shoes.

Nicky did his own stint in the Corps and now he was sheriff of Beaufort County. It was not as simple as that, but that's the way it turned out.

It was a time of great change, days of seething criminal revolt by operators large and small. From an African-American backwater, fishing, truck farming, and a few military paychecks, one sheriff, three deputies, scant fifty years later, Beaufort County was Ohio license plates, strip malls, strip joints, big box stores, pot-heads, crack-heads, coke-heads, strong-arm robberies, rapes, assaults, arsons, dog bites, dogfights, burglaries, assorted cuttings and shootings and continuous vandalism.

One chief deputy, three lieutenant colonels, three majors, three captains, five lieutenants, upwards of one hundred grunts in fast Fords, twenty-two million dollars spent each year.

Summer and winter, officers were well dressed, khaki or green according to the seasons, military fatigues, tall green socks, safari shoes, Kevlar vests and strapped up with every device from billy sticks to Tasers. Didn't seem to matter much, though. They all made more overtime than they could stand. The dopers got side-tracked, career criminals got fast-tracked. But alas, twice that number of cops could not have kept up. Several hundred felonies pending, a score of missing persons, and a dozen murder investigations gone cold. You never seen such.

Give a sensible man a choice between a good dose of the clap and being sheriff of Beaufort County, a sensible man would choose the clap every time. At least there was a cure for that. The sheriff had run unopposed the last three elections.

And now Deacon Limehouse sat at his desk, Bible in hand. "Sheriff, this sort of behavior is simply not acceptable." He smiled like an undertaker smiles when he slips you the bill. Deacon Limehouse owned the Ford dealership and sold insurance on the side. He was the agent for the sheriff's health policy.

"Mr. Limehouse," the sheriff began, then paused. "It's Deacon, right?"

"Yes, sheriff, Deacon, installed by the Ugandan Anglican Church."

"Uganda? That's a-ways off, ain't it?"

"Make straight through the wilderness a highway for our God," the deacon said.

The sheriff wanted a cigarette but he could not smoke one, not even in his own office. The only thing that kept him sane these days was a wry sense of humor. He got to hide it most times, sending his majors or his captains out to meet the press. But it busted loose sometimes one on one. "Reckon He'd need a bridge, too," he said.

"Such things are not to be taken lightly, Sheriff," the deacon sniffed. "The Ugandan Church blesses me with direct apostolic succession."

The sheriff tucked his gaze and shuffled papers upon his desk, the report of the incident in question.

"Your deputies broke down my door. They disrupted a gathering of the Elect."

The sheriff fanned through the papers again. "Seems a neighbor reported a hostage situation."

"Hostage situation?"

The sheriff passed the papers toward the deacon but the deacon did not take them. "Transcript of the 911 call. Of course, your neighbor's name has been redacted. Apparently, your group was walking around the living room with their hands in the air?"

"Sheriff, they were waiting on the Comforter!"

The sheriff's daddy let his religion slide, being no Greek Orthodox Church handy. The sheriff briefly wondered if they might be raffling a quilt. A cult? Why else would a man walk around in circles with his hands up waiting on a quilt. He reckoned it was better than handling snakes.

"The Comforter, the Holy Spirit, Sheriff," the deacon said. "And your men broke down my door."

"Deacon, I think I can arrange to have that repaired."

"Sheriff, that door was two hundred and fifty years old."

"Oh," the sheriff said.

After the deacon left, the sheriff went into his private bathroom, turned on the fan and lit a smoke. When he was done, he flushed the butt and looked at himself in the mirror.

He needed a shave. On the mirror was a sticky-note he had written to inspire himself in moments of indecision. Only the Mexican cleaning girl knew it was there and she did not speak English.

"How stupid can you be and still breathe?"

The sheriff was a good man in a tight spot. He mopped his face, cleared his throat and went back out again to meet his next appointment.

There is something free and fine about a spring tide. Spring tides do not always happen in the spring, though sometimes they do. Moon and sun and sometimes wind conspire, most-times predicted, sometimes not. The sea seems to spring its normal boundary, flinging itself upon the beach, up into the saltmarsh and even flooding the dunes and the scrub woods thereabouts. The great waving fields of Spartina grass are inundated until just the tips show above the water. Moonlight, it looks like tarnish on pewter; daylight, a green fuzz upon a mirror of the sky.

Hampy was no longer undercover, so he tucked his hair up under his DNR cap, strapped up his Glock and used the agency boat. He stopped in Beaufort and picked up Doretha from the Codes office. She was a humorless raisin of a woman come to Codes from Child Support Enforcement, a heavy smoker. Her teeth were yellowed and jumbled toward the front. She tried to hide them when she spoke but some words made her look like a cross between a piranha and a mullet. She was also licensed to carry a pistol, a Glock, just like Hampy's.

She had a bundle of papers beneath one arm, information on a new bulb, light humans could see but turtles could not.

They were technically not legal as such things were not contemplated when the regulations were written. But she would offer the resort a deal. If they bought two or three hundred bulbs at forty bucks a pop, she'd let the whole matter drop. Doretha did not know if the new bulbs would screw into the existing sockets or if the entire facility would have to be re-wired. It never crossed her mind.

They launched the boat at All Joy landing, where the road played out a little east of Bluffton. Hampy knew the story and he loved it, the dance hall in the old days, the rooms in back for ladies of negotiable affection. That's where Old Man Pinckney ran scotch whisky ashore, offloading English ships into fast forty footers with double-mufflered twin Packard V-8's. They hauled it to Ridgeland and cut it with local shine, slipped it into a boxcar on the Atlantic Coastline Railroad, New York City bound. The sheriff nabbed a load whenever he got thirsty but most got through. No matter what, All Joy patrons got first run at liquor and women.

Old Man Pinckney put his money into the wild swamp along the lower reaches of the Savannah River, as drearisome spot as you'll likely find. Everybody thought he'd lost his mind until the engineers came looking for ground to dump dredge spoil when they deepened the channel. Then Pinckney retired to a farm outside Levy, where he grew okra and raised black Angus cattle, sat on his porch and gave the finger to all his friends as they passed by. His boy got the county mosquito contract and a half hour after they found his spray plane loaded with marijuana down on Harris Neck, he called and reported it stolen.

There was Savage Island and Bull Island and a twisting creek between them, where the live oaks threw their mossy limbs out over the river, where sweet shrimp crackled in little side creeks and alligators lounged in the low tide shallows. It was a tricky piece of water but Hampy knew it and he buzzed around the turns at full throttle while Doretha did her best not to smile.

The turtle girl met them on the dock, the one who called in the complaint, the girl on the video, the great beauty. She swung her hips and walked with her toes out while sun and river wind worked magic in her hair. Sure as shit, she was pregnant, plugged, four, five months gone.

JESUS AND CLINICAL DEPRESSION

Carla smoked dope during both her pregnancies and her kids were smart as whips. That gave her hope. But she wouldn't drink. Jeanie would drink but dassan't smoke dope, as they piss-tested her at work. But between the two of them, they got it done.

"Big hands and big feet," Jeanie said, "you reckon he's got a big dick?"

They were talking about Hampy. Women will talk dirty when menfolk aren't around. Some women can cuss paint right off a wall.

"Hush," Carla, said, firing up another joint, "you fixing to get me wet."

They were down in Carla's singlewide with the plywood porch on the marsh side of the island, blistering hot when the August afternoon sun bore down, drafty when the winter winds blew, all she could afford. The rent wasn't too bad but summer and winter, the power bill gave her hell. Jeanie got another rum.

"You still get wet pregnant?"

Carla rose from her chair, did a little knee-bend, cupped her crotch and grinned. "Whoo-hoo, girl," she hollered.

"Shut up," Jeanie said. "You get more than I do."

"Your own damn fault," Carla said.

"He sure chewed new asses on them sons-of-bitches."

"Talk about ass? He took you outside, what was that all about?"

"Ships."

"Ships? Uh-huh. You talked about ships?"

"Yes, ships."

"Bullshit. I seen you smiling and wiggling. What you know about ships?"

"Not a damn thing."

"You see that hair?"

"What hair?"

"Tucked up under his hat?"

"No."

"Must have been watching his ass."

"Shut up."

"OK."

Carla reached across the table and grabbed Jeanie by the nape of her neck. She had good strong hands. She moved to kiss Jeanie on the lips but she did not. The women looked eye to eye, but then let it drop. They were lonesome women on a lonesome island, no bridge, no yogurt, no yoga and they did the best they could.

Phantom backed the van into the jailhouse sally-port. There was a woman behind four inches of glass. Like a drive-through bank teller, she handled deposits, withdrawals and returns. Earphones, a throat mike, butched-off bottle blonde with a bad run of acne.

"Clear?" she asked.

"Clear," Phantom said.

A single double-throw switch controlled both doors. Only one could open at a time. Phantom left the van running. A jailor brought out a cuffle of prisoners. Six of them, shackled at ankle and wrist. Orange jump suits, loose slippers, dreadlocks. The jailor gave Phantom the handcuff and leg-iron keys. "I'd watch my ass if I was you," he said.

"Where we headed boss?"

"Shut up," the jailor said, "you'll find out soon enough."

Shit, Phantom thought, *Shit. Where the hell is Hampy?*

The men clattered into the van, stumbling and cursing. Phantom unlocked one set of leg irons and cuffs so they would sit on two seats. The inside door closed and the outside door opened. Phantom put the van in gear.

"Hey Boss," somebody hollered again, "where we goin'?"

"Wal Mart," Phantom said.

The sheriff fingered the accountant. He was pushing sixty, an overweight, wheezy wine connoisseur, a little light in his loafers, everybody said. The missing couple was in their forties, drank Bombay and Perrier. They worked out at Gold's four nights each week. The couple was not the only thing missing. Their funds were half a million short.

Wasn't too hard to figure out.

Two days after the accountant was named as a person of interest, the neighbors called 911 and deputies broke down his door. Dead in his bathtub, carved up with a serrated steak knife, a suicide note on a bed sheet, hieroglyphs in blood.

The body went to the Medical University in Charleston for post mortem. Alcohol, Benadryl and antidepressants. The bedsheet and the computer were seized by SLED, sent off to Columbia for translation. SLED, the State Law Enforcement Division, answered only to the governor. Black Crown Vic Fords and blue suits, red ties, machineguns and satellite telephones.

Nicky Jackitus met the press. The suspect embezzled money, and when confronted, killed the couple, then himself. *We are trying to find the bodies to bring closure for the family.*

But there were no bodies, not a whisper of DNA anywhere, no hair, no blood, nothing. Just an empty holster at the account's house and no pistol to fit it. And there was no family to which to bring closure, or at least not much of one. The woman had a brother in Atlanta, that's all.

When the press asked about the multiple stab wounds, the sheriff said, "It was a very motivated suicide."

There was the briefest flurry of discussion. The press interviewed several psychiatrists, none of whom could medically differentiate between ordinary suicides and very motivated ones.

When the press asked how the woman's Mercedes got halfway across the island several hours after she was presumed dead, the sheriff said nothing at all.

Pressed by a pesky reporter, the sheriff called him Nancy Drew.

"What y'all in for?" Phantom watched the faces in the rear view.

There was an immediate shaking of heads, a collective rolling of eyes and an explosion of explanation. Bad checks, child support, marijuana, each excuse punctuated by an extensive invocation of motherhood and fornication.

Traffic was backing up. Phantom reached over his shoulder and grabbed the first man he got his hands on. Phantom had a good right arm. He grew up throwing cast nets. He kept one eye on oncoming cars while he wrenched the man forward, nearly over the seatback, clinching him nose to nose. The second man howled and the last grunted as the leg-iron chain ran out of slack.

"You tell me what you're in for!"

"Armed robbery, boss!"

"That's better. Now how 'bout the rest of you sons of bitches?"

There was a new and sudden litany of confession, robbery, home invasion, manslaughter, all awaiting trial in District Court before being shipped off to the big house in Columbia. Phantom shook the man until he slobbered but the van never crossed the center line.

He turned the man loose and the man sunk back into his seat with a gurgle and a sigh. "We will visit the shoe section. Each of you will grab a pair of white rubber boots. You hear me?" He talked while he drove.

"Yessir!"

Phantom pulled into a handicapped slot and the men rattled out. "Each of you will also pick up a three-pack of white socks," Phantom hollered. "Then we will proceed to the hardware section. There each of you will pick up a shovel."

There was a mighty howl of complaint, like Phantom had just undone the Emancipation Proclamation. "You will choose a shovel with a fiberglass handle. Then we will stop at paint supplies where each of you will purchase a three pack of face masks. At checkout, each of you will be allowed a pack of cigarettes."

Phantom paused. There was a vague murmur of ascent. "Generic cigarettes, regular, light, or menthol."

Then he turned to the biggest man in the gang, floppy liver-blue lips, a gold tooth the size of a postage stamp and a neck bigger than some men's waists. He'd never live long enough to sit down in the electric chair.

"And if any one of you so much as farts," he poked a finger in the center of the big man's chest, "I'm gonna kill you first. Any questions?"

"But how we 'spose to try on boot with these here laig iron?"

"I reckon you know what size," Phantom said.

"But, Boss, you can't truss no Chinee size."

"You gone truss 'em today," Phantom said.

"Boss, you is crazy," the big man said.

Phantom just grinned. He took the big man's paw in his hand. His own was only big enough to go around half of it. He looked the big man in the eye and the big man knew he was not fooling.

Wal Mart superstore, ten AM, sufficient to pray up Noah's flood all over again. Mexicans who could not look an Anglo in the eye, women with babies at the hip, babies in strollers, women with both. Women with classic bowling pin physiques, double chins, triple chins, no chins at all, women brown, black and white, each pushing great cart-loads of white bread, marshmallows, diapers and Twinkies, other children and scrawny husbands in tow. Husbands followed as long as they would, then eased outside, taking their turns rotating across concrete benches, the rough surfaces worn smooth by their bony denim asses, hooking over cigarettes and sucking them down to the bitter ends.

Jesus wept bitter tears, the Good Book says, when He beheld the masses from the temple steps. He would have wept again here, yea, He would have fallen down in clinical depression.

The first shall be last and the last shall be first. But it was hard to figure out who was who when this motley multitude fell back before Phantom's clinking and shuffling procession. The clientele stood wide-eyed and drop-jawed, and then they parted like the Red Sea before the Children of Israel.

Phantom fingered his Glock. The round in the chamber was a Golden Talon hollow point. It would make bloody Jell O of a brain, heart, or liver, but it would not go clean through a man and kill some other poor son of a bitch three aisles down, trying to get a battery for his '76 Toyota. Next round up was full metal jacket. It would shoot clean through any Toyota.

Pray up a flood? The Lord said there would be a fire next time.

Where the hell is Hampy?

LIBERALLY AND EQUALLY UPON CONVICTS AND CONSTABLES

Hampy caught up with Jeanie in the barn. She was bringing a horse inside, a roan stallion, lathered with sweat. "You're back?" she asked.

"Yes ma'am. Just need to ask you a few questions."

The stallion snorted, pranced, tossed his head, snorted again. Jeanie clipped on a second lead rope, cross-tied the animal in the barn alleyway. "I thought what's-her-name got it all sorted out." The barn smelled of shit and horse piss.

"I talked to codes, she said she would fix it."

"Doretha? No ma'am, this ain't about turtles."

Jeanie uncoiled a hose, twisted the spigots, checked the temperature of the flow. She smiled the faintest gator smile and worked her free hand into a terry mitt hanging from the top rail of the stall.

"You read the paper?" Hampy asked.

"No," she said. "History by the time we get it."

"Two missing, one dead," Hampy said.

Jeanie ran the hose down the horse's back. Warm water coursed down his flanks and belly. She soaped his back with the mitt. A mockingbird chirped out in the yard. "Three dead."

"You think?"

The stallion struck the concrete with a front hoof, tossed his head again and commenced a mighty erection. It was hot pink, stout as a man's forearm with a neon knot like a fist at its head. Water flew as the stallion slapped it impatiently against his belly. Jeanie squatted and soaped the horse's cock. "A person can't help but hear things," she said, following her hand with the warm water hose. The stallion rolled his eyes, flared his nose, curled his upper lip. "Unk, unka, unka," he said. No male on earth breeds with such a ferocious gusto. Mane hair from the mare he had just bred still hung from his teeth.

"Oh yeah, I bet that feels good," Jeanie said, "yeah, so good," casting her eyes at Hampy. "Got to clean him up good," she explained, "he's got to do it all over again in the mornin'." She turned off the hose, dropped the mitt and fixed Hampy with her pecan eyes while she patted the stallion's neck. "Poor thing," she said with a great and sincere sadness, "he gets so excited, I have to help him put it in."

That's when Hampy knew he was in big trouble.

"Takes both hands," she said.

Carla waited till she heard the steady rhythm of the bedstead against the trailer house wall. The children were off at school and would not be home for hours. She slipped her shoes, peeled her pregnant stretchy-front britches. She shucked her shirt and her breasts were wonderfully swelling ripe. She threw her clothes at Paula Deen, who was drawling along about peach cobbler on the flat screen. Carla palmed the bottle of cooking oil from the kitchen counter.

She crept to the bedroom door and just before she turned the knob she thought, *Like eatin' peanuts naked on the courthouse lawn. Girl, this is just too damn good to pass up.*

Nobody wants to talk about it anymore, how two hundred inmates and twenty-two officers bogged the stinking mess for three days, that commercial landfill south of Savannah, that square mile, six hundred and forty acres of the vilest filth, forty feet high. How the gulls and buzzards hovered and shit liberally and equally upon convicts and constables. Nobody notes the heat strokes and the expensive medivacs as the cell-bound convicts succumbed one by one. Phantom went out with six men, came back with five and he did better than most. The big man was laid up in Savannah, handcuffed to his bed at Memorial Hospital at considerable public expense. He would likely recover.

The van stunk so bad Phantom left it running in the jailhouse sally-port, AC up, windows down. He slipped beneath the overhead door just as it closed, walked out on the concrete apron, spit, gagged and vomited, then called a cab on his government cell phone.

When he got home, he burned his clothes.

Phantom sat in his skivvies and watched the flames from his easy chair. He grabbed his remote and surfed the channels for ten minutes, nothing on. Then went to his laptop and in ninety seconds he knew exactly where Hampy was, the bastard.

That new phone. Phantom chuckled. No such thing as a free piece of ass.

Hampy's number was pre-programmed. "I know all about that island pussy. Holler at me quick and there won't be no trouble."

No way was Hampy going to call that number on the state phone, hell no! He used his personal cell instead.

"Hey, Big Boy," Phantom answered, "so sweet of you to call."

Looking after loggerheads wasn't as much fun as it used to be. Five or six years before, the girls loaded up sweet rolls and a carafe of strong coffee and hit the beach just after each glorious sunrise, Mid-May to Mid-October. When they found a crawl, they would stake it, date it and wrap the area with orange flagging tape. If a crawl looked like it might be inundated by the next spring tide, the girls would poke and probe till they found the eggs, sometimes nearly two hundred the size and crinkle of ping pong balls. They would gently place each into a pail, ease up the beach to higher ground, then rebury the clutch. They set rough courses with a pocket compass. A jolt or even the slightest rotation of the bucket could kill the eggs.

But now the DNR required every nest to be probed so no false crawls would pollute the data. Five days after each projected hatching, each nest would have to be excavated and inventoried—hatched shells, un-hatched eggs and dead hatchlings entered into an online spreadsheet. Live but trapped hatchlings were noted, liberated and released four feet from the waterline as it was thought the memory of the smell of this beach would bring them back to it a quarter century later.

Then all information was daily uploaded to a server maintained by an international team of sea turtle scientists and conservers. Jeanie and Carla did all this for free and even without the head-butt with the resort manager, it was getting to be a pain in the ass. And now there were rumors next year, or maybe the year after, they would be given needles and syringes to extract a small amount of white from one egg in each nest for DNA testing. After years of research and protection, the DNR still had no real idea of the size of the breeding population. It might take another ten years of genetic mapping but this was a sure way to find out. After rescuing turtles from a chlorine swimming pool, both women loathed the thought of sacrificing even one egg in the Name of Science.

Calibogue Sound, three hours after sundown, dark thirty. Nothing but a quarter moon and the distant lights of Savannah to light the sky and sea.

The boat was nose to the wind, drifting down the tide, running seaward at two knots. A twenty-three foot lap-strake hull with a fifty horse Yanmar diesel, the Coast Guard Auxiliary aboard. Six men and every man-jack drawing Social Security.

Yankees from Sea Pines, mostly, and they did not have much else to do. Complimentary boat inspections most summer weekends. No horn? No throwable device, buckles busted on your life jackets? You got a fix it list before you got a ticket. Every so often they were called out for training.

A sudden halogen light over the east like a rising star and the whine of an incoming chopper, a jet turbine gathering to a whomping roar. A man on the boat popped a red flare and threw it overboard and the wind from the rotors blew it back aboard and there was a serious scrambling as the flare went over the other side.

Foul weather gear is for rain and sideways spray, but rotor wash comes from beneath.

The Coast Guard Auxiliary was wet from their bung holes to the parts of their receding hairlines when Oscar hit the water.

Oscar was a man-sized and man-weight dummy. Oscar was a naval term for Man Overboard.

The men wrestled Oscar aboard and the chopper hovered, blasting them with wind, jet wash and salt spray.

The chopper dropped a basket. The men strapped Oscar into the basket, the chopper winched Oscar back aboard and slanted and whined off towards Savannah.

The boat turned back to Harbour Town.

Six minutes and forty-eight seconds, a successful rescue, the papers said.

"My ass was bogging a landfill with a gang of cutthroat negroes," Phantom said, "and you were out chasing tail."

They were in Hampy's pickup, at the usual rendezvous along the banks of the blackwater Edisto. "I don't recall homicide investigations as part of your job description," Hampy said.

"And I don't recall pregnant pussy as part of yours."

Hampy choked on his beer.

Phantom shot him a wicked grin, mimicked the intro to the old radio show, "Who know what evil lurks in the hearts of men? The Phantom knows."

Hampy pulled the cell from his belt, tossed it to Phantom. "Take back your goddamn phone!"

This time Phantom giggled. "I got you in my sights, big boy." He reached into his pocket, palmed a digital recorder, lay it on the dash. Hampy could hear the steady thump of the bedstead against the wall, then Carla squealing, "Can you feel the baby? Can you feel the baby?"

"Yes, yes!" His voice was so husky with lust, he barely recognized himself.

"Ah, the wonders of technology. You check your voice-mail lately?"

"On which goddamned phone?"

"Your own damn phone. I know you damn sure didn't give those wenches your agency number."

"You bastard! You hacked my voicemail!"

"You might be glad for it someday." Phantom paused, took a pull off his brew. "You might be glad for it right now." He reached for the recorder, thumbed fast forward.

It was Jeanie and Carla, talking fast and both at once. Hampy couldn't make out what they were saying. But they were all spun up and they wanted him on the island, now.

"Put the boat in the water." Phantom said. "I'll meet you at All Joy in an hour."

"You're coming too?"

"You goddamn right. I ain't letting your ass out of my sight." Then he added, almost as an afterthought, "Never seen a pussy on the scrap pile yet, man that stuff is tougher than hog snout."

"What in the hell does that have to do with anything?" Hampy snorted.

"We got one dead, two missing," Phantom said, ticking each phrase off the fingers of his right hand. "We got unknown boat traffic at odd hours. We got a sheriff who don't give a damn. And now we got two hotties and you just banged 'em both, at the same time I am persuaded to believe. And they got infrared and they are calling you on the phone?" Phantom's thumb was still free so he wiggled it around under Hampy's nose. He stroked it obscenely with the fingers of his other hand. "Maybe you ought to tell me?"

Hard to catch Hampy flatfooted but he was flatfooted now. His head was spinning and he was too stunned to do much more than mumble and cuss.

"And come out of that green," Phantom said, "you're undercover again. And you will report to me and only me." Phantom patted the recorder in his pocket. "You understand?"

Hampy did.

WILTING WIVES AND WHORES

Phantom brought the shovels. He had more than they needed, more than he would ever need again during his entire lifetime, he hoped. He was indifferent to shovels before, but he actively hated them now and even the sight of one raised the bile in his belly.

He took them to the carwash first, blasted them clean as he could, front, back, all the way up the handles. He nosed them when he was done but they still smelled of the landfill and the bile rose in his throat when he got the scent. He retched and spit, threw four into the back of his truck. It was a green heavy-duty Ford like Hampy's, but marked with the agency logo.

Phantom drove south and he was seriously pissed. There was a copy of the *Island Packet* folded upon the dashboard, the current issue. The South Beach Dredging Association had just been awarded a permit to dredge the marinas on the south end of Hilton Head. Three hundred thousand cubic yards of toxic muck to be deposited at the mouth of Calibogue Sound, where the tide would hopefully sweep it away.

It was the first permit for near-shore disposal in history. Environmentalists were raising billy hell, bottom paint, marine toilet residue, benzene from fuel dock overflows. Didn't matter. Boeing was sponsoring the next big golf tourney and their corporate yacht could only float on high tide. Low tide, the silt would foul the heat exchangers for the air conditioning, the executives, their wives and whores would wilt. City Fathers needed prime time video of the yacht on national TV. They draped the stern of the missing couple's yacht with a painter's drop cloth. It was still moored pending settlement of the marina bill and the estate, so there were no videos of that.

Screw the environmentalists, Phantom did not give a good goddamn. A middling porpoise will shit as much as five men each day. The Department estimated there were five hundred or so in the waters hereabouts. Run the numbers and you got twenty-five hundred men crapping in the river. Yes, bottom paint was bad, so was spilled fuel, but there was less oil than ever, now that most everybody had given up on two-strokes, which blew a fine oil mist out the exhaust.

No, he didn't give a rip about any of that, but this was the destruction of a crime scene.

They might have used a dragline, a bucket half the size of a Toyota at the end of a crane. A dragline would get the job done, and if there was a bushel of bones in the bucket, they would have spotted it maybe. But no, it was a hydraulic dredge, a giant egg beater churning the bottom like a blender. Bones would shatter, rattle through the pump and into the pipe, the shards pumped away onto Barrett Shoals, two miles to sea, out of sight, out of mind forever, perfect end to the perfect crime.

The girls picked Phantom and Hampy up at the dock in a rusted-out golf cart that smoked and backfired but ran. Freeport Marina, gateway to the island, the sign said.

"We found something. Some asshole dug up a nest." Carla explained in their ramble to the beach. "We thought it was some Mexicans looking for eggs. They think," she managed the faintest smile, "turtle eggs will give them a hard-on."

"That's all we need," Phantom said, "more Mexicans with hard-ons."

There was one paved road from one end of the island to the other. Carla drove and Jeanie sat in the passenger seat. Hampy and Phantom sat in the second seat. It faced backwards. They could not see where they were going but they could see where they had been.

"But then there was plastic," Jeanie said.

"Plastic?"

"Black plastic."

"A turtle don't lay plastic," Phantom said.

"No shit," Carla replied. The girls did not know Phantom, did not like him either, at least not at first.

The oak trees spread their limbs over the road, branches to the left and right meeting overhead, twigs intertwining, locking together like fingers of lovers in love till the road looked like a long green tunnel. They drove till the over-loaded cart began to wallow and mire in the soft sand. The cart finally lurched to a stop. "End of the road," Carla said, "gotta hoof it from here." Carla walked duck-footed along the beach. By that time they were down to just two spades. Two Phantom left in the carwash bay, a second pair in the truck at All Joy. Now Hampy carried one, Carla the other. "Goddamn, this shovel stinks," she drawled. "Y'all been digging up an outhouse?"

Different folks did it different ways but Jeanie and Carla did it like this: Three one-inch square surveyor's stakes driven in a triangular pattern around the nest site, twenty inches, two feet apart. Each stake bore a twist of orange flagging tape at the top. One stake bore the official US Fish and Wildlife Service Keep Off and Away warning, the final stake with the nest number, date of laying written along the stake with indelible marker. All info, including a GPS fix was also recorded on paper and uploaded daily to satellite.

These stakes were thrown this way and that and the sand churned beneath. Carla approached the site like Moses might have approached the Burning Bush the morning after, very carefully. On her knees, pregnant ass high in the air, sweeping blow sand left and right with generous sweeps of her long strong arms. When Phantom saw the first flutter of black plastic, he said. "Back off y'all and everybody shuck your shoes."

Hampy shot him an evil look. Phantom returned his best weasel grin.

"I know you," Hampy muttered soon as he got the chance, "You fixing to throw these gals to the fishes."

They were all barefooted now, Hampy and Phantom with their warden shoes strung around their necks with the laces. Carla and Jeanie had their flip flops run down into the tops of their britches as they drug ten kilos of cocaine back to the golf cart.

Phantom shrugged. "What the hell man? We got an ass of free coke. We got two and a half women and I'll bet there's a six pack of Bud back at the shack. We is barefoot and we drawing wages the whole time!"

"You are an impossible ass," Hampy said. "You'd bullshit the hangman."

"Trust me," Phantom said.

"Oh, I trust you," Hampy said, "to get me into a crack where I got to shoot my way out."

Another weasel grin. "Listen to me, big boy, and any gunplay will be entirely recreational."

"Where we taking this shit?" Carla asked.

Hampy pointed at Phantom. "Ask him."

"Them sonsofbitches sure gonna be surprised," Phantom said, "when they realize they ain't taking this toot back from a bunch of hippies."

So they lay the perfect trail. When the sack threatened to wear through and dump the toot in the dirt, Phantom hoisted it into the seat, then occasionally struck the road with the point of the spade instead.

Phantom took first watch while Hampy crawled off to sleep with Jeanie and Carla. No racket there, everybody too freaked to fornicate. Phantom couldn't keep the kids straight. The younger slept on the foot of the bed in the near bedroom, the other curled in a sleeping bag at his feet. The driveway was white sand, a quarter mile long and all lit up by the moon, coming now full in three nights. Meandering through the dark wax myrtle and palmetto scrub, the sandy track was as cool and bright as beer sign neon. Ghost, coon, possum, mink or man, if something moved, he would see it.

A wisp of blonde hair and a freckled nose peaked from the sleeping bag.

"I'm Cassie," the girl said, "momma calls me Cassandra when she gets mad."

"OK, Cassandra, you go back to sleep now."

"You called me Cassandra," the girl said. "Are you mad at me?"

There was a flash of dark within the dark at the end of the drive, a quarter mile distant. "Oh no," Phantom thought, "oh hell no!"

But he said, "No honey, I'm not mad at you."

"What's your name?" the girl looked at him like a spaniel.

"They call me Phantom," he said.

"Oooh, that's scary, but you aren't scary."

Flickering movement again, closer this time.

Phantom unsnapped his holster.

"Do you have a little girl?" Cassie asked.

Phantom lay his hand upon her head, smoothed her salt air curls, kept an eye on the driveway. If he ever had girl children, they'd be grown up, haired over and gone by now. "No, honey, now please go to sleep."

"You don't have a little girl, and I don't have a daddy," her eyes would have wrung tears from a May River ballast stone, cast off a sailing ship so long ago. "Will you be my daddy?"

SHALL WE GATHER AT THE RIVER?

The double-wide was dark and Phantom sat back to a dark wall. About forty yards to the south was a derelict goat shed or chicken coop, now full of rusty, flat-tired bicycles and a lawnmower or three in various states of disrepair. Just before sunset, Hampy scratched up a bunch of lamp cords, robbed the light bulb from the fridge and hung it in the shed. Anybody slipping up the driveway would sneak on that dim light.

Phantom kept his eyes on the driveway, reached for Cassie's head in the moonlight. "Yes, honey, I'll be your daddy."

"Oh goody," she squealed and ran in place beneath the covers. "I love you Daddy."

"I love you, too, Cassie. Now I need you to do Daddy a big favor."

"Sure Daddy."

"I need you to cover up in your sleeping bag and don't come out or even make a peep till Daddy tells you to. Okay?

"OK, Daddy."

Phantom leaned back in his chair and wrapped softly on the bedroom door.

Hampy grunted.

"You got your boots on?"

"Yep."

"Your turn, big boy. Go get 'em."

Phantom waited on the signal, a quick flash from Hampy's blue lens LED. Blue was a good color, not too bright and it lit up the faintest trace of blood. Right handy when a man or deer was leaking and on the run.

Two men were face down in the sand. They looked like cops, jump boots, green fatigue britches, green short-sleeved shirts. Hampy had them cuffed tight, hands behind their backs. One man had a knot the size of a guinea egg alongside his left ear. "Get me some ID on these sons-of-bitches," Hampy said.

One of the men kept trying to speak, but his mouth was full of sand. "Eff, Eff," was the best he could do.

Phantom put his foot in the middle of the first man's back, worked his wallet from this back pocket, did the same to the second. He flipped open one wallet, then the other as Hampy played the light over the contents.

Phantom whistled, shook his head. "Oh Kemosabe," he said, "looks like we just busted the DEA."

"I don't know who in the hell you clowns are," the first man said, gagging and spitting, "but you just mucked up a perfectly good cocaine investigation."

"Don't you Kemosabe me," Hampy snapped, then turned to the men on the ground. "South Carolina DNR Enforcement! Somebody buried that dope in a loggerhead nest and we got jurisdiction!"

"This is a Federal matter and we have jurisdiction. Now take off these cuffs and return our sidearms!"

"Excuse me," Phantom interrupted, bending almost to their ears, whispering and curling his lips like a demon. "but I don't believe you boys is in any position to argue fine points of the law."

Hampy put his foot back on each man in turn, half his considerable weight between their shoulder blades. He could have broken each man's neck with a swift kick to the back of the head but he did not. He unsnapped their magazine holsters and retrieved the magazines. They were Glock, government issue, double stacked nine millimeter, stuffed with full metal jacket. Shit ammo but it would kill you dead as hell up close. Hampy dropped the magazine from each pistol, threw them into the bushes. Glocks were carried with a round in the chamber, ready to go, point and pull the trigger. Hampy cleared each gun, dropped the rounds into the sand, twisted them from sight with the ball of one foot.

"We fixing to turn you loose," Phantom said. "But you make one wrong move, and you'll be deader than James Freaking Garfield."

Hampy uncuffed them while Phantom held them at gunpoint. The men struggled to their feet, compulsively rubbed their wrists, the way men do when the cuffs come off. Hampy had them cinched up tight and there was more rubbing than usual. The man with the lump on the head spit sand in a series of dry wracking coughs. The one who could still talk said, "Our sidearms please."

"Sit down," Phantom said, "and come out of those boots. Socks too."

"What"

"You heard me!"

"You'll go to jail for this!"

"Don't count on it bub. You're in South Carolina now."

Hampy and Phantom stood in the moonlight and watched them go, hobbling through the sandspurs, limping and cussing, dragging ten kilos of toot. "Sorry excuse for cops," Hampy said. "You got that receipt?"

Phantom patted his shirt pocket, paper torn from the little spiral bound notepad all cops carry.

"Come on, the girls will be worried about us."

"Worried about *you*," Phantom said. "They don't give two shits about me." He pointed down the driveway, "Just you keep your eye on those bastards. One of them might have an extra magazine stashed somewhere."

"I'll keep my eyes peeled. But we handed 'em their asses. Reckon they got a generous plenty of us already."

Jeanie and Carla peeked around the bedroom door, faces etched with worry. "It's okay," Hampy said. "Y'all go on back to bed. I'll tell y'all all about it in the morning."

"Oh shit," Phantom was looking at the receipt for the dope. He turned it over; he turned it upside down. "Oh shit."

He passed it to Hampy. It was blank, not a name, not a number, not a squiggle. "You're a dumb-ass," Hampy said.

"What you mean, dumb-ass? I saw them write. You saw them write. What in the hell is this? Some kind of Boy Scout freaking disappearing ink?"

"Dumb-ass," Hampy said, louder this time.

There was a stirring in the sleeping bag on the floor between them. Little Cassie stuck her head from beneath the covers, rubbed her eyes, yawned. She rose to her feet, stood between them, her curls even with Hampy's buckle. The men paid her no mind.

"We came all the way over here. We dug up dope, we hauled it here. You used these girls and these children as bait. Internal Affairs are gonna be all over us in about three emails." Hampy had to stop and catch his breath. "We could have got our asses shot off besides. And oh hell no, that was not enough! Then you gave it away? Dumb-ass!"

Little Cassie wound up and punched Hampy square in the scrotum. He doubled up and his scant breath left him.

"Don't you call my new daddy a dumb-ass," she said.

Hampy fought to find his wind. Nothing ever hurt so bad.

Phantom scooped her up and she buried her face in the nape of his neck. "Yea, out of the mouths of babes and sucklings...." He said.

"I never knew you to be so God-damn religious," Hampy finally gasped.

"Whenever it suits, brother, whenever it suits."

"Bastard," Hampy said.

"Oh Daddy," Cassie squealed. She tightened her grip on his neck.

Deacon Limehouse led the faithful down to the river. It was a diverse multitude, nubile daughters of his parishioners, a pimply faced boy or two among them. Hand in hand he walked with Pastor Ben Williams of the St. John Come Out the Wilderness Baptist Church, a concrete block edifice on about two miles down Squire Pope Road from US 278.

Ben Williams was a three-hundred-pound school bus driver who took up preaching in his spare time. He carried a six-foot peeled oak stick in his right hand, worn and twisted as the staff Moses carried before Pharaoh. It could not turn into a snake and eat up the Pharaoh's snakes but it would fend off moccasins, stingrays too and steady his considerable stance on a muddy bottom. Widely known for his righteous ways, his unshakable convictions, spirited sermons in his rich baritone, Pastor Ben gave up his day job entirely and attracted congregants from Savannah to Barrel Landing. The pastor brought along his own small covey of initiates, blooming brown girl twins, and a scrawny knock-kneed boy.

The twins were Miss Ernestine's nieces and when you get invited to a river baptizing, you better damn well show. Hampy watched the proceedings from a mound of oyster shells beneath a riverside live oak, forty yards upstream. It was after first frost now and he wore his winter fatigues and sidearm, kept his hair beneath his cap. Showing the flag, he called it, but about now he did not know which flag he was showing.

The deacon and the preacher and all the children wore white and they were followed by aunts and grandmothers, neighbors and cousins, two hundred strong. The deacon and the pastor's robes were store bought, but as the Apostles Creed proclaims "one baptism for the remission of sins" it would be a one-shot deal for the children. Their robes were simple bed sheets, holes cut in the middle for head and arms, like little ghosts up for Halloween, waists secured with a hank of rope, whatever was handy, frayed poly crab trap rope mostly, an anchor line or sash cord, each tied with an expert square knot. Hampy knew Pastor Williams had put his loving, school bus driving hands to each one.

Hard to find a place for river baptizings any more, the creek banks all grown up with houses and condos and dockside restaurants the way they were. They were down at a raggedy old shrimp dock, broke off piling, loose deck boards, four of the old boats tied two deep at the T-head, two more snubbed off to old live oaks and rotting away at the shoreline. The riverbank was paved with oyster shells, packed hard as concrete by the passing of many feet. And each time the Pastor and the Deacon walked it, they wondered if it might be the last.

"Shall we gather at the river," Pastor Williams boomed, walking in slow cadence with the song, striking the ground with the butt end of his staff, "the beautiful, beautiful river?"

The congregation took up the song, approaching the tide in slow procession. "Shall we gather at the river, that beautiful, beautiful river…"

And then the Pastor lent his voice to the crescendo, "… that flows from the throne of God!"

They never baptized at low tide, lest everybody would bog down in river mud. They never baptized on the rising water, even if nearly high tide, as the river would wash your sins away and then the tide would change and they would come drifting back and get on you all over again. The proper time was just into the ebb, even if only ten minutes, so the river would carry your sins to sea and they would never bother you again.

The congregation stopped at water's edge but the deacon and the Pastor locked arms with the nearest children and the children all locked arms with one other and they all waded out hip deep. The water was not so cold but is seemed cold and the girls' nipples puckered and prophesied of the women they would someday become.

There are two species of Baptists, the Primitive and the Missionary and all Baptists hail from one or the other, even if they won't admit it. The Primitive look to Isaiah, where the prophet says God knows you from the womb. Heaven or hell, a done deal before your daddy even shucked his jeans. So, there wasn't much sense in preaching to strangers. The Missionary Baptists look to Matthew where Jesus says He won't come back till the Gospel is preached in every land. The Pastor was Missionary and the Deacon was renegade Episcopal, wrestling The Word.

Pastor Williams laid his hand on one of the twin's head and bellered out, "Do you accept Jesus Christ as your Lord and Savior?"

"Oh yes," the twin said in her reedy little girl voice.

"Then I baptize you in the name of the Father...." He plunged her beneath the water, fetched her up again by the hair. The twin spit and sputtered. "And the Son...." Down she went again. "And the Holy Ghost." When she came up the third time, there was a hank of yellow ski rope over one shoulder. At first Hampy thought her homemade sash had slipped but then something moved beneath the water and the twin screamed, "Oh Lawd, de debil got me!"

Then somebody on the banks hollered "Gator!" and Hampy drew his Glock and ran.

There was a collective shriek and a rush from the water and those in the crowd nearest the creekbank drew back instinctively. Hampy waded to his knees, grabbed the rope with his off hand while he kept his pistol at the ready, his finger tight on the trigger for a breathless moment then something moved again and a corpse floated to the surface.

There was a low harmonic moaning from the crowd, like a chorus of whistle buoys way out at sea, then another shriek that paled the first and a great stampede of young and old up the riverbank. Doors slammed, clutches smoked, gravel flew and dust hung heavy in the air. In two minutes there were six canes, two walkers, assorted vestments, a yellow rope with Hampy on one end, a corpse on the other.

Most of a corpse, anyway. It looked like it had been in the river for a week.

JAIL TIME IN TEXAS

It was a single-story concrete block building on a concrete slab, painted the color of the trees behind it. There was a tin roof rusted the color of the sand in the parking lot. A blink in the road, you might miss it even if you knew it was there, one hundred feet off US 278, the only way onto the island and the only way off. Incessant traffic hissed and rumbled, ready-mix concrete trucks, US Foods semis full of Chinese shrimp, Indonesian crab, grouper from Ecuador, which passed for local seafood for the tourist trade. There was Mexican day labor hanging off the backs of raggedy pickup trucks, fifty miles an hour and a man could get killed just stopping in for a Nehi soda.

There were sodas for sale but nobody bought them. There were a couple packs of yellowing and viscous sandwich meat, a moldy block of cheddar, stale Nab crackers and a jar of jawbreaker candy. Nobody bought them either. The walls inside were plastered with civic awards, some framed, others thumb-tacked onto a fly specked wall.

Hampy sat on one side of a card table and Jeremiah Jenkins sat at the other. Folks who knew him called him Cooter. Cooter Jenkins was a patriarch among the First Families, the Barnwells, Draytons and Simmons, the descendants of the slaves who endured, multiplied, prospered and remained. They stuck together like Masonic brothers and maintained a code of silence under official interrogation or even casual inquiry, a cutting or a shooting, everybody knew everything but nobody said nothing.

Cooter Jenkins was also a notary public, with legal power to transfer motor vehicles, to marry, to file a writ of divorce if presented with the proper papers. But mostly he was kin to all the cab drivers and he was right convenient to the highway. Liquor on Sundays, reefer or women any day, Cooter Jenkins was your man.

He was a waif, almost a ghost, perhaps not long for this world, knobby elbows and shuffling shoes. He wore a sweat-stained Panama with a rattlesnake headband and his broad dark glasses hung a full inch off either side of his face.

"And what might you want with me, Mister po-leese man?"

"Who that man I pulled out the river?" Hampy asked.

"What man?"

"You know what man."

"You mean that white man with the po-leece britches and new boots?"

A semi threw on his jake-brake and juttered to a stop at the traffic light, brakes squalling, tires hopping. The window glass rattled in the frames.

"How you know bout new boots?"

"Read 'em in the *Islunt Packer*."

"I read the *Island Packet* too. Didn't say nothing about boots at all. And how you know I pull him out?"

"You jus tole me, Mister Po-leece man"

Hampy kept a thousand in small bills in his glove box, a contingency fund, government money. The department sold a million plus hunting and fishing licenses each year, at an average forty bucks a pop, but that all went straight to the general fund and the legislators doled it out as they pleased. There was an annual parade of "ologists" wanting to get paid. Biologists, ornithologists and even archeologists got in line and Enforcement got the scraps sometimes. The Thin Green Line, they often joked but it was no joke. The cash was strictly accounted for monthly, even while undercover.

Hampy reckoned this was government business and if it wasn't yet, it was damn sure gonna be quick. No ID yet on the corpse, but Hampy knew exactly who he was and who likely killed him too. He bought a round of golf at Sea Pines, never played it but left his government phone locked in a locker room locker. Nobody knew where he was. Now he lay five hundred onto the table, pushed it across to where the old man could reach. Cooter Jenkins palmed it like a casino boat blackjack dealer, and broke a grin to shame a mule.

"Now, Mister Po-leese Man, what can I help you with?"

Hampy knew better than to run the corpse by him again so he said, "How bout that couple?"

Cooter Jenkins was nearly blind. You might not know that at first, so long as he was in his concrete block sanctum along US 278 where he knew where everything was. He turned his menu this way and that, passed it to Hampy. "You read um for me."

They were at Frankie Bones, an Italian joint of the north end of the island, not far from Cooter Jenkins' cheese, baloney and whatever shop. There was a black and white art-deco hexagonal tile floor, a genuine brass rail at the bottom of the marble-topped bar and the walls were covered with large format black and white photographs, Mickey Mantle, Frank Sinatra, assorted mayors and mobsters and Marilyn Monroe in various states of dress and repose. A single candle flickered on their table, the old man's dark glasses caught a reflection and looking at his eyes was like looking back a quarter-million years.

Cooter Jenkins worked his throat, his Adam's apple rising and falling like an old-time pump plunger. "Can't a nigger get a drink?"

"They done been axe you." Hampy lapsed into Gullah, easy to do now. "You say you ain't want nothin'."

"All I seen was sto-bought. Didn't have no scrap iron."

"You want scrap iron, I'll get scrap iron. I'll be back in two shakes. You sit tight."

"You buyin', I ain't flying," Cooter Jenkins said.

They called corn liquor scrap iron from when they had a voodoo sheriff in the old days. He'd look you in the eye and *axe* you a question and if you tried to lie you would slobber all over yourself. Bootleggers hauled homemade hooch from Hilton Head and Daufuskie to Savannah, hiding cases of Mason jars in boats and pickups beneath clattering piles of rusted car fenders and hoods, blunting any official inquiries with, "Nuthin' but scrap iron, suh." They all swore the sheriff was bullet proof too. And his blue sunglasses could see a still clean through a tin roof.

Riley's Fine Wine and Spirits was half a block away, just the other side of the drug store and travel agency. Hampy nodded at the hostess on his way out. She was a tiny thing, pushing fifty and wearing it well, with a wasp waist, tight black britches, hair like a new penny and an ass that was worth two hundred bucks in tips any weekend shift.

Riley's Fine Wine and Spirits, one till for beer, another for spirits. A coalition of Baptists and bootleggers kept South Carolina dry for seventy-odd years. And when they gave it up, they did not give up easy. A wine store could not sell liquor, a beer store could not sell liquor and a liquor store could not sell beer. No signs, just a red ball of a size prescribed by law, a minimal affront to the Elect. No sales after legal sundown so the closing hour would be two minutes early or later each day, depending on the season. No sale on Sunday, no sale on election day, no sale, no sale.

Even after liquor stores were legal, there was no legal liquor by the drink for the next forty years and when tippling was finally permitted, bars could sell only mini-bottles which the customers had to pour themselves. Bar owners did not mind too much, as it was an easy way to track inventory but environmentalists raised hell about all those little bottles in the landfills and Mothers Against Drunk Driving disapproved of the full ounce and a half pour. Cutting back to a single ounce, would save lives, they reckoned.

There was a handicap spot square in front of the door, so the tipsy red nosed and blue-haired Yankee matrons would not have to totter far for their Safire Bombay. Riley's was staffed by a burly black kid in dreadlocks and the place smelled like he had just blown a joint in the back room. Hampy chose a quart Mason jar of Georgia Moon, legal shine as it bore state and Federal tax stamps. He paid cash and walked back to Frankie Bone's.

The hostess saw the jar. "Oh sir...."

Hampy flashed his badge, pinned to the inside of his wallet.

"Oh, oh...." She stammered. "Oh that's alright, sir. Enjoy your meal."

Hampy sat down, slid the bottle across the table. "I'll get you a glass," he said.

Cooter Jenkins took the jar, twisted the bag till it would not touch the rim and grinned. "This come with a glass, don't it?" He loosed the lid and took a generous long pull. He smacked his lips. "Jesus take the wheel!"

Hampy went back to the menu. "We got salad and we got bread." Hampy squinted too, too many years on bright water and blinding white beaches. "They got she crab soup."

Cooter Jenkins took another drink. "That Yankee she crab ain't fittin' to slop a boar hog."

"They got chicken cacciatore."

The old man's face lit up. "Chicken cacciatore? Won't that get you jail time in Texas?"

Cassie and little Lucinda sat bare foot on the end of a dock in a little green water side creek as the tide inched its way toward full. Little Lucinda had her index finger on a crab line, Cassie stood ready with the net. Cotton net twine wrapped around a stick jabbed into a crack between the deck boards, a chicken neck and a galvanized washer for a sinker on the other end. Late October but the water was warm and the creek held crabs. The Spartina cane was gold as grain for the harvest and the little cedar hammocks stretched off toward the curve of the world and shone like emeralds in the afternoon sun.

"Think I got one," Lucinda whispered.

"Bring him up real slow."

Lucinda inched the line, one little girl palm at a time. When Cassie saw the crab, she came up from beneath it with one long deep stroke of the net.

"Jimmy crab, jimmy crab," the girls squealed as the first of the evening's catch went scrabbling around the bottom of their basket. Lucinda put the bait back overboard, sat down. Tide was high enough now so the very tips of her toes could reach water.

"I got a new daddy," Cassie said.

GIVEN THE TIDES AND PREVAILING WINDS

Legally Dead.

The boat could be sold and the marina bill settled. The woman's brother could sell the Atlanta house and collect the significant life insurance.

But such things are not to be rushed into. There are legal standards for being legally dead. A person, or persons, must be absent from his, hers or their home or usual residence and such absence must be continuous and without explanation for a proscribed length of time, nine years in some states, seven others. Such absence must be accompanied by lack of long-distance communication to those most likely to hear from the potentially legally dead and diligent but unsuccessful inquiries as to their whereabouts must be made. And finally, the person or persons must be notified via certified mail that they are about to be declared legally dead. The legal pleadings for being legally dead must be heard by a probate judge or if the matter is contested, General Sessions Court.

There was no contest and a scant six months after they turned up missing, the Calverts were legally dead.

There is legally dead and there is just plain dead and the sumbitch Hampy pulled out the river at the baptizing was dead as hell. Ed Allen was county coroner and he had the body in the morgue, yet to be positively identified, blue and cooling with a number on a tag on his left big toe.

Hampy, the preacher and the deacon were subpoenaed and testified at the coroner's inquest. All were placed under oath and interrogated but since the coroner never thought to ask if Hampy had ever seen the man before, Hampy was able to avoid perjury.

Being coroner of Beaufort County was almost as bad as being sheriff. Ed Allen had bodies stacked like cordwood. If a body was unidentified and unclaimed thirty days, it was cremated and the ashes put in a box and the toe tag taped to it. There were sixty-three such boxes stacked on a table in his office closet dating back to the late 1980s. Ed Allen was a five-foot four-inch black man. He said when he took the job, he was six two and white.

The corpse in question was stitched through the upper torso three times, a nine millimeter or maybe a thirty-eight. No powder burns on the body, so lethal wounds came from six, ten feet away. No slugs or shell casings were recovered. There was an older contusion behind his left ear. There was water in the lungs, so he may have still been alive when he hit the river, Ed Allen said. Given the tides and prevailing winds and the condition of the body, he likely died within two miles of the site of recovery.

It caused a minor flurry of interest. But as half a dozen bodies drift ashore each year, not so much.

Ed Allen may have been stumped and Nicky Jackitis may have been stumped, but Hampy figured he knew the story.

"You killed that sumbitch," he said.

They were back at the usual rendezvous along the Edisto and looking into Phantom's eyes was like looking into the eyes of a canebrake rattlesnake. His left eyelid twitched just a little. He worked his jaw muscles and finally broke into his usual weasel grin. "Maybe some folks deserve killing," he said.

Deep down in the Fall now, the gum trees had lost their leaves to a litter of yellow and gold drifted here and there among the bell-shaped trunks. Cypress were knee deep in water and bare limbs stretched to heaven like they were thanking for the past season and praying up the next. The oaks were still green and dropping fruit. The frogs were gone and the gators denned up and the coons, deer and wild hogs were scrabbling after the last of the acorns, splashing through black water like they were used to it, which they were, higher than usual that year. Wood ducks wheeled and whistled through tall timber, *Poo-wee, poo-wee.* They were eating acorns, too.

And then Phantom gave him the stink-eye.

Hampy just came off a sweet little bust, shrimpers selling shrimp, run afoul of the fine print, willfully and knowingly. You can bait shrimp with fish meal and take a forty-eight quart cooler home each day, but you dassn't sell it which they did.

Hampy scruffed up scruffier than usual for the occasion, looking hungry, dipping Copenhagen, spitting liberally and drooling on his shirt till it looked like a canvas in the Guggenheim Museum. By and by some folks from Georgia asked if he needed a little easy money and he did. He was wearing a body cam and was wired for sound.

"Fresh local shrimp." Magic Marker on an upended tomato box, ice from the Kangaroo Express. The shrimp stunk like fishmeal, but the Yankees did not know any better and Hampy helped them sell a couple hundred pounds out the back of their pickup alongside US 17, south of Hardeeville, the last high ground before the Savannah swamp.

They gave Hampy fifty bucks long green and a six pack of Bud Lite. He asked for a can of Wintergreen Long Cut dip but did not get it.

Then he gave them a ticket for $1,146.75.

The grand was the fine and the balance was court costs.

He dumped the last few shrimp in a side ditch for the coons and crows.

He smoked dope with them too, but did not charge them with that.

And he paid for his Wintergreen himself.

Hampy was still wearing wire when he had that Come to Jesus talk with Phantom. Damned if he was going to get caught flat-footed again.

But Phantom wasn't having it. "Come out of that shit and turn the Goddamn sound off."

Hampy did. He twitched and un-tucked, laid the tangle of wires and the matchbook black boxes on the hood of the Chevy.

Phantom eyed the equipment for flashing red or green LED's. "Now you listen to me! I didn't kill that bastard but how do I know you didn't kill him yourself?"

That was bullshit and both men knew it. "I coulda killed him dead as hell but that would have left a very messy scene. You just don't kill a man on beach sand above the tideline, dumbass."

"You remember the last time you called me dumbass?"

Hampy did and his testicles hurt just remembering. "But if you kill a man on a dock and pick up the shell casings, it's pretty clean."

"Damn straight. On the deck or a boat too. But I didn't."

Hampy tried not to think about going for the gun. He knew Phantom would see it in his eyes. "So you didn't kill him? Who did?"

Phantom shrugged, kept on grinning. He could out-grin most men, most animals too. "May I humbly suggest it was the last man to see him alive?"

"No shit, smartass."

"Smartass? I been promoted?"

Hampy reached across the hood and fetched up Phantom with a rattling good slap. Hampy had a long arm and a heavy hand and the pop echoed through the timber. Phantom's eyes went blank, rolled up into his head. His eyelids fluttered like dying quail and Hampy had half a second to move. He rounded the fender in a flash, tackled Phantom and threw him square on his back in the soft leaf litter. Phantom bucked and flayed his legs, trying to reach Hampy's neck but Hampy leaned forward and pinned Phantom's gun arm with his left knee.

"Now what?" Phantom gasped.

Indeed. After 911, an assault upon An Officer of the Law while on duty was an automatic felony. An assault upon An

Officer of the Law while on duty by another Officer of the Law also on duty was another. Five years for the first, three for the second, no voting, no guns, not even a box of .22 shells until personally pardoned by the president. Obama was president that year, fat chance.

Phantom writhed and bucked again, managed to get one leg around Hampy's neck, peeled him off and sent him rolling. Hampy flipped onto his belly, came up with his Glock. Phantom did too and the men lay on their stomachs ten feet apart in the musty leaves, each with his pistol sights square between the other's eyes.

"Hey big boy," Phantom wheezed, "we having fun yet?"

"Bastard!" Hampy spit leaves. "Go back to counting fish and ducks!"

"Too late for that, Kemosabe," he panted, struggling to catch his wind. "You know they are running toot into Harbour Town. Two gone missing and now two dead. "

Phantom laid his Glock in the leaves, took his hand slowly from it. Hampy did the same. Neither man made a further move.

"Did you know, perchance, there were two dirty wine glasses in that accountant's kitchen?" Phantom spit out an acorn. "You can bet your ass the sheriff will eventually get off his ass and match the DNA to ol Blue Boy, very privately, of course. He's likely done it already. He might not know who the hell he is but he'll know it's the same man. Maybe I smell Russians. Maybe I smell Jamaicans." Phantom whispered like he was afraid the owls might hear.

"You got your head so far up your own ass, you can't

smell nothin'," Hampy said.

"Hell, you say!"

"There weren't no wine glasses."

"Bullshit. I seen the crime scene photos."

"And I seen the list from the SLED lab. No wine glasses." Long pause. "That's a felony," Phantom said.

"Maybe he liked his wine so much, he used two glasses?"

"Sounds like something the sheriff might say."

"Whoever it was, they cut that poor faggot up fourteen ways from Sunday, blood on the walls, blood on the floor, blood on the ceiling. He was laid out real uncomfortable like, head at the small end of the tub, face right under the spigot. But maybe he wasn't queer. He spent a lot of money down at the Diamond Club."

The Diamond Club, Russian money some said, a gentlemen's club with scant gentlemen in attendance, where you paid your money and took your choice. The girls rotated through, Atlanta, Charlotte mostly but hardly any Miami strippers. They were a bit standoffish at the beginning of each month, somewhat more liberal as the nights bumped and ground on. There was a joke among the yachties and dock monkeys and if it wasn't true, it should have been:

"A man asked if he could put a Coke bottle up my butt."

"Oh no! What did you say?"

"Plastic or glass?"

That was Dunnigan's Alley. There were roads on Hilton Head, avenues, parkways, drives, courts and cul-de-sacs, but only one alley.

"Did you know there was another note?"

"I didn't," Hampy said. "What did it say?"

"Says, 'Dennis is not the only one, keep looking.'"

"Why in billy hell would anybody leave a note?"

Phantom shrugged. "Remember Son of Sam and the Zodiac Killer? But this ain't your average broke dick psychopath. You know who found him?"

"Paper said neighbors called the sheriff."

Phantom gravely shook his head and a leaf that had stuck to his hair wafted to the ground. "Two lawyers," he said.

Cooter Jenkins said the Calverts weren't dead and Phantom wasn't sure. It was two AM and Hampy was back at his shack with the curtains pulled fooling around on his laptop. His personal computer, not the agency's. Google Calvert and there were ads for cheap whiskey. Google Missing Calvert and there were a series of newspaper articles about a liquor heist in Kentucky. He went to the *Island Packet* homepage and did a search. His computer clicked, clacked, rattled and whined. One thousand, two hundred and sixty-three hits. He grabbed a note pad and pencil, padded to the kitchen for a cup of coffee.

This was going to take a while.

About three thirty Hampy hit the wrong button and came up with this:

"An aging mobster who stayed mostly in the shadows for decades by adhering to the Mafia's strict code of silence was acquitted Thursday of charges he helped plan a legendary 1978 Lufthansa heist retold in the hit film "Goodfellas."

A federal jury reached the verdict at a Brooklyn racketeering trial where it heard testimony that portrayed

80-year-old Vincent Asaro as a throwback to an era when New York's five organized crime families comprised a secret society that committed brazen crimes and settled scores with bloodshed.

Asaro, whose father and grandfather were members of the secretive Bonanno crime family, "was born into that life and he fully embraced it," Assistant U.S. Attorney Alicyn Cooley said in closing arguments. His devotion to the Bonannos "was as permanent as the 'death before dishonor' tattoo on his arm," she added.

The defense accused prosecutors of relying on shady paid cooperators, including Asaro's cousin Gaspare Valenti. They argued that the witnesses had incentive to frame Asaro to escape lengthy prison terms of their own.

"These are despicable people," defense lawyer Elizabeth Macedonio said in her closing. "They are accomplished liars."

At trial, prosecutors described how Asaro rose through the ranks and developed an "unbreakable bond" with the more notorious James "Jimmy the Gent" Burke, the late Lucchese crime family associate who orchestrated the hold-up at the Lufthansa cargo terminal at Kennedy Airport. Taking the witness stand last month, Valenti testified that Asaro and Burke killed a suspected informant with a dog chain in 1969 before ordering Valenti to help bury the body.

Valenti also testified that Asaro drafted him for the Lufthansa heist, telling him, "Jimmy Burke has a big score at the airport and you're invited to go."

When he learned about the mountain of $100 bills and jewels taken from a Lufthansa vault, Asaro was "very happy, really euphoric." Valenti testified. "We thought there was going to be $2 million in cash and there was $6 million."

Prosecutors claimed he collected at least $500,000 from

the score but had a gambling problem and squandered it away at the racetrack."

It had absolutely nothing to do with the issue at hand, yet at the same time, everything. Keep your mouth shut, kill a potential witness to terrorize the others, and you will walk. Or at least until your own bad habits caught up with you.

God had all the time in the world.

But Hampy did not.

HE COULD SMELL HER MELT

"You ain't told me yet why them sumbitches buried toot in a turtle nest," Hampy said. Miss Ernestine just brought their orders, ribs for Hampy, grilled chicken breast for Phantom, fries, cole slaw and two draft beers, Palmetto Pale Ale from Charleston. It wasn't quite as good as Sam Adams, but Sam Adams was a damn Yankee. She didn't say a thing about the corpse at the baptizing and Hampy knew better than to mention it. She would not look either of them in the eye, so they knew she was thinking about what none of them would say.

They were out of uniform and unarmed, at least at casual glance. Hampy had a snub-nose Smith and Wesson .38 in a hip pocket. It was a hammerless model and it came up quick and never snagged.

Phantom twisted his head this way and that, massaged his jaw. "Damn it, you didn't have to swat me so freaking hard." His cheek was mottled like a pizza and his right eye was bloodshot, red, blue and purple all around.

"Hit a man hard enough the first time, you never got to hit him again."

"Asshole."

"You lucky I didn't break your damn fool neck." Hampy peeled a rib from his rack, bit into the fatty end. Juice ran down his chin. "You ain't answered my question."

"Anybody ever tell you pork is bad for your health?"

"I never seen a pork chop kill nobody yet," Hampy said. "Keep talking."

"Just bad luck in the dark." Phantom peppered his cole slaw. Restaurant cole slaw was not worth a shit less a man doctored it first. Curry powder worked best, but they did not have it here. "Got something in my pocket for you."

"A Beretta .25?" Hampy asked.

A .25 wasn't nothing to a raging crackhead, but it hurt plenty, others testified. Slugs were short and unstable, tumbled around inside the chest. Made a mess.

Phantom broke his weasel grin, albeit a weak one. "No, Kemosabe, gun iron is heavy, paper is light. The paper is pun-top the Beretta."

Hampy took another bite. "Pass it over."

It was not a warrant for assaulting an officer while on duty, but a tear from the *Island Packet* no bigger than the butt end of a two by four. A single paragraph under 'Local Happenings'

"Coast Guard conducts Man Overboard drills with local Auxiliary."

"Check the date."

Hampy did. "Those stupid bastards tried to land toot in the middle of a drill?" he asked.

"Bad luck, like I said and nobody comes ashore with ten kilos, even twenty. More buried out there, sure as shit. Want to go look?"

"Hell freaking no," Hampy said. "You go. You got family out there, as I recall."

"Bastard," Phantom said.

Dunnigan's Alley, one AM, almost closing time. Hampy wore a get-up he bought online from Men's Wearhouse, a charcoal gray Joseph Abboud Survival Suit with "wrinkle resistant water repellent stretch fabric for a man on the move." It fit pretty good and the pants pockets were deep enough for his pistol. He unbuttoned the top of his shirt and slipped his tie a few inches. He loosened the knot and skewed it to the left. It was bright red and easy to see in dim light. He had a secret stash of Cuban Cohibas and he put one in the coat pocket, turned it to where the label showed. He took a traveler of Jim Beam from beneath the seat and splashed a little on his cheeks like cologne, took a nip, sloshed it around his mouth, then spit. He thought better about it, took another generous slug and swallowed. It burned good all the way down.

He quoted Cooter Jenkins, "Jesus take the wheel!"

It wasn't much of a joint, like a two-story Dollar General with a gable front and double doors with a diamond-shaped transom above, an architectural approximation of a spread-legged woman. A Mercedes two-seater parked beneath the live oaks, a couple of wore-down pickup trucks sagged in the slanting late night moon, a limo idled beneath the pines, running lights on, headlights off. Styrofoam cups rattled in spirals and circles on the sea wind, freshening now on the tide change, and the gravel crunched beneath his feet.

Hampy could not see but he knew them by their breaking. Brown glass with fragile screw on plastic tops, small as the last bone in your baby finger, perfect for a bud, a gram, or whatever your junkie-ass needed, snap, crackle and pop.

There was dreamy bluesy saxophone jazz on the Muzak and a willowy long-haired blonde hostess at the door. She wore low-cut white satin, slit up one side nearly to the point of her lovely hip. "Good evening, sir. Will you be joining us for breakfast?"

"Breakfast?"

"Yes sir, we have an all you can eat buffet at two."

"Ah no, just a couple of drinks."

She smiled like a gator. "Don't want to lose that buzz, right?"

Hampy grinned back. "No ma'am, got to take good care of it."

"Have you been here before?"

"No ma'am."

"My name's Sherri. You don't have to call me ma'am."

"No ma'am."

She giggled, jiggled, her nipples got hard. Hampy cut a fine figure, indeed. And he smelled like bourbon and money. "We have continuous floor shows and private party rooms upstairs for your enjoyment. Follow me, sir. I'll find you a good seat."

She led the way. *Lord help me, Hampy thought, if the dancers look this good.*

"And you don't have to call me sir."

Sherri stopped in mid-stride, pivoted on a stiletto, pointed her index finger and looked him square in the eye, a little flushed at face, neck and shoulders. "And what can I call you?"

"You can call me Hampy," he said.

She shot him another gator smile. "I don't know anybody named Hampy."

"You don't know me either. Yet."

He could smell her melt.

Three girls this time of night and one was busy upstairs. Hampy heard the laughing and thumping, boys from the limo most likely. Mexican staff would clean it all up with wet towels when they were done, spray Air-Wick here and there. Next.

It worked like this: Three stages, three poles, three sets of alternating lights, white, red and a blue so deep it was almost purple, a rotating disco ball throwing butterflies of bright on sweet female flesh, easy chairs all around for gentlemen's repose. But only one pole going that night. If a gentleman showed any obvious interest in any particular gyration, he was tagged for further inquiry. The first girl was brunette and shaved and waxed to a goatee, the second was blonde and completely bald. She pouted at Hampy, top and bottom. It was hard not to look.

"Would you like a dance?" She hovered over his chair.

"I don't dance," Hampy said.

She tossed her hair, brushed it away from her eyes. Her breasts were small but her nipples were like two strawberries in cream. Hampy had a fifty handy but she had no place to put it.

She tucked in the only place she had.

Hampy knew the feeling, the rush of blood, the aching in the jaws, the headache like eating ice-cream too fast. She put her knees on the arms of his chair and waved her sex six inches from his nose. She smelled like cheap jasmine perfume and woman. She spoke thick east Europe, like her mouth was half full of marbles, gurgling, heavy on the vowels. "And what would you like, beeg buoy? You like my poosey?"

"Talk dirty in Russian," Hampy said.

Goon and dancer, same accent. Half a man high and two men wide, the goon caught up with him at the bar, shiny bald, dead eyes with a mean scar across his left cheek. No dancer, just Hampy and the goon.

Hampy had a drink and a gun when the goon shrugged his coat off his shoulder till the cuff covered his right hand. The flash of steel and the crisp snick of a cheap switchblade shank.

"You have greatly upset my employee."

Jimmie Hoffa said "rush the gun but flee the knife." And Hoffa knew what he was talking about. He was president of the Teamsters Union and likely killed Bobby Kennedy and maybe Marilyn Monroe too, but the mob finally wearied of him and turned him into a hubcap. Some fifty years later, the FBI still gets tips and regularly digs up yards all over Detroit in vain.

But Hampy neither rushed nor fled. He kept his hands at his sides and backed away slowly. "I am so sorry, my friend. This man was like a brother and I have always wanted to know more about his passing. We were classmates at Georgia Tech."

Oh shit, the accountant did not go to Georgia Tech, John Calvert did.

Maybe the goon missed it, maybe not. His dead eyes never said. Oh Jesus, he was good.

"It would be very good for you," the goon said, "if you would let the dead be dead."

Cassie saw him coming had met him halfway up the drive, sand flying from her tiny bare feet, "Daddy! Daddy! Daddy!"

She flew into his arms and buried her face in his neck. "I knew you would come back to me." She was crying.

Little Lucinda sucked her thumb and big-eye peeked from behind the screen door.

"Mommy, Mommy, Daddy's home!"

Cassie brought a Mason jar of tea and ice. She snatched a sprig of mint from beneath the trailer house steps, pinched it and floated it on top.

"I love you Daddy."

And the sun slipped off toward Savannah. There on the plywood porch on the south side of the trailer house on the south side of the island in the early winter afternoon the spires and domes of that glorious and tragic city glowed across the wide water like the New Jerusalem. But it was not the New Jerusalem. It was the murder capital of the southeast. Liquor, dope or women, you took your chances in Savannah.

Phantom smoothed a map upon the table, where oh where was the rest of that dope? One man survived the drop. Would he come back and snag the rest? Or did he just kill his partner, take the dope in hand and run? Coke rots the brain, feeds greed. Phantom figured he would come back for it, if not now, later but Phantom could not wait forever. He'd been out of pocket too long already and the colonel would get wind of it and he'd be called to Columbia to make account. If he told the truth, the colonel would assign the case to the DEA and send him back to counting fish and ducks. They were ten days off the next new moon, high tides and black-ass dark, a good time to bring a small boat ashore. Cassie sat on his lap, played with his hair. It was a government cut, but she twirled it whenever she could find it between forefinger and thumb.

Carla put her face to the screen. "I don't recall inviting you," she drawled.

"Official business, ma'am."

Phantom perused the map. *Now where in hell did they bury the rest of it?*

Cassie went to fetch up more tea. "Oh Daddy, come quick," she hollered. "Mommy's sick!"

Carla wasn't sick, she was in hard labor, bent nearly double, knuckles white on the kitchen counter edge, the linoleum floor slick with amniotic fluid. "Oh, Jesus," she panted.

Jesus, indeed. Back in Sunday school they called Jesus the Great Physician, healing epileptics, making the lame dance, giving the blind 20-20, driving demons into swine, even raising the dead, but they never said He was an obstetrician. Didn't matter. Jesus was a long way off and Phantom was on his own.

He put one arm around her ribcage, gave her some support. "We got to get you to a doctor."

She smiled weakly. "Doctor? We got no doctor. Call Jeanie, she'll come get the kids."

The lights flickered once, twice, then failed. That's the way it worked on these islands. The pine hit the high-line, fire flew, the breakers tripped, came back on and tried to burn it clear. If it couldn't clear the line by the third jolt, it shut down till the crew got there with their chainsaws.

Jeanie cried out, sagged and another great rush of amniotic fluid spattered and pooled at their feet. It smelled like a shallow saltwater pond in late July.

Phantom had been scared to Jesus death on a regular basis, but nothing like this. "Cassie!"

She was right at his elbow. "Yes, Daddy?"

Phantom thought fast. "I need you to do Daddy a favor. Grab a bucket, get your sister and get on down to the beach. See what you can find Daddy."

"Ok Daddy," she paused, teared up. "Is Mommy going to die?"

"No Cassie, Mommy is not going to die. She is having a baby."

"Oh goody," Cassie said.

Wasn't even time for the bed. Contractions upon contractions, Phantom eased Carla to the floor. "I got to pee," she said.

Phantom reached for the sink to wash his hands. The tap signed and gurgled out a drop or two, no power, no water, no juice to run the pump. Phantom wiped his palms on his game warden britches, sat between Carla's knees, his butt suddenly wet from nubbins to bung.

"I got to pee!" she said again.

"You lay right there. I ain't fishing no baby out of no shitter." He grabbed her sweatpants, slid them from beneath her hips, peeled them off her legs, no panties. He threw them aside, splat. Her sex was swollen like a cantaloupe.

"Holy Christ," Carla moaned. "Shit! Get a shovel handle and knock me out!"

But there was no shovel handle close at hand. Contractions, sweating, screaming, cursing. When she began gnawing at the cabinet corner, Phantom threw her a dish towel and told her to wad it between her teeth instead. But she ignored it. He put another on the floor between her thighs to catch the baby. It was cleaner than the floor, maybe. Five minutes, ten, he could see the top of the head, blue with a fine thatch of black hair, plastered tight to the skull, more showing with each new push.

"What we got?" she panted. "What we got?"

We hell, Phantom wanted to say. But he said, "I can't tell by the head!"

"It's coming, it's coming, it's coming! Oh Sweet Jesus, it's coming!"

And a baby slid out onto the dishtowel, like a fat-back mullet sloshed from a ten quart pail, blue as a corpse from the river. *He's dead, he's dead!* Phantom thought. He grabbed the child, rolled it onto the side and cleared mucus from its mouth with his thumb.

It was a boy. The child shuddered, took a deep breath and loosed a plaintive cry like a new born lamb. One breath, two, he was pink as a piglet.

"We got us a boy!" Phantom hollered without realizing the pronouns. "He got all his fingers and toes!"

"He's crying, give him to me."

The cord, oh shit, the cord!

Phantom untied his left boot, dug for the folding knife in his left pocket. Six inches of bootlace, a clove hitch and a snick and the child was free. He passed the him to his mother. He was crying now, full throated, the most piteous sound Phantom had ever heard.

"Oh, my baby," Carla said. She thrust the boy beneath her shirt and the boy nosed for a tit. His cries gave way to muffled grunting when he found it. The placenta was coming, two sudden heaves, an arch of her hips, like a liver from a fresh killed deer. Knots and strings of blood, like roadkill on the trailer house floor.

Carla struggled to her feet, blood coursing down her thighs, eyes lit with holy fire.

"Great God, wait a minute!" Phantom said.

He grabbed a beach towel, followed her to the bedroom, turned back the covers, lay the towel on the center of the bottom sheet. He piled pillows atop one another, pulled the quilt over mother and child right up to momma's chin.

The lights flickered, the fridge rattled and hummed as the power came back on.

The screen door slammed. "Daddy, daddy!" Cassie yelled, "We got conch for supper!"

BEYOND THE CALL OF DUTY

For a century, Charleston was the center of the known universe, where locals claimed the Ashley and Cooper rivers met to form the Atlantic Ocean. But as run-away slaves, indentured servants on the lam, free persons of color and Revolutionary bushwhackers began peopling the red clay upcountry hills, there arose any manner of legal disputes, civil and criminal. Litigants and suspects often rode three days in mud and rain, some in shackles and all miserable, to sit before a jury of bluebloods and Frenchmen in Charleston, which fueled resentment and gunfire. There might have been a Second American Revolution, then and there, but in 1786 an upcountry senator introduced a bill that was approved by the legislature to create a new state capital everybody could access with equal difficulty.

Pre-dating Washington, DC by one year, Columbia was,

after the ancient pueblo in Taos, New Mexico and Savannah, Georgia, America's third planned city, 400 Blocks in a two-mile square along the banks of the Saluda and Broad rivers, divided into half-acre lots and sold to speculators and prospective residents. Buyers had to build within three years or face an annual penalty. They laid out streets one hundred and fifty feet wide, believing a mosquito would starve to death making the flight. They paved the streets with wooden blocks which floated out with each heavy rain.

Some years into the process, Thomas Taylor, the former owner of the land, paid a visit. "They took one pretty good plantation," spake he, "and made one sorry-ass town."

It took one hundred and eighteen years to build a proper statehouse. It was still unfinished when General Sherman shelled the city in February 1865 from his vantage in Lexington County. The statehouse was the only building visible above the treeline and it received most of his attention. Two shells crashed through the windows and exploded inside. Seven others bounced off exterior granite walls. The scars are marked with bronze stars to this day.

Sherman was afflicted with an obsessive-compulsive disorder and dis-union was the ultimate disorder. He harbored an especial hatred for the city as the First Baptist Church was the site of the Secession Convention of 1860. When a Yankee mob approached the sexton and demanded directions to the Baptist church, he directed them to the Washington Street Methodist, which they burned instead. Another mob attacked a bronze statue of George Washington with brickbats, breaking off his cane. When admonished by their sergeant, they replied, "Sorry Sarge, we thought it was just another god-damn rebel." Later that night, Sherman burned Columbia to the ground and blamed it on retreating Confederates who were long gone by then. Yankee historians still insist it's true. But hardly any believe, then or now. When the smoke cleared and the ashes settled, the good citizens of New York sent Columbia two fire engines after there was nothing left to burn. After 9-11, Columbia sent two fire trucks to New York. Everybody knew what really went down.

War is hell? In July, the only thing between hell and Columbia is a screen door.

But it was early March when Phantom was summoned before the Colonel. He figured the jig was up, too long out of pocket with nothing to show but a newborn boy, damn that child.

The *Island Packet* ran the story. They got wind of it when Carla finally went in for a post-partum checkup and Volunteers in Medicine emailed Social Services. Birth certificate? Who was witness to the birth? All government emails are public property in South Carolina and reporters hovered over in-boxes like buzzards over road kills. They called his land line three nights, but he had caller I-D and never answered. Hard to run a story without comments from him, but they ran it anyway. Maybe the Colonel thought the boy was his.

Second floor, Rembert C Dennis Building, Assembly Street. Rembert Dennis was elected to the state assembly in 1939 after his daddy E. J. was shot down by Sporty Thornley over moonshine coming out of Hell Hole Swamp. E. J. was in cahoots and his murder was an inside job. It worked like this: E. J. controlled the constables and they would arrest any moonshiner upon his orders and seize the whiskey. Then E. J. sold the whiskey to his own bootleggers. He was also a lawyer and made more money through attorney's fees and "tokens of appreciation" due upon acquittal, the cost of doing business in the Hell Hole.

But the racket could not last forever. Sporty laid a dou-ble-barreled shogun loaded with buckshot across the hood of his car pointed in the Senator's general direction and, Damn-It-All, the gun went off all by itself. Sporty was a veteran of the Great War, a tubercular with the intelligence of a turnip everybody said. Due to some murkiness of the exact circumstances leading to the Senator's demise, Sporty drew a life sentence rather than the chair.

Rembert said he did not want his candidacy to be thought of as a way of avoiding the draft, so he promised to immediately volunteer if he lost the election. He was doing it for his dead daddy, and for his momma too, as women were unelectable in those days. He did not have to worry, he was more Democrat than Jesus and he won every election right up until his retirement forty-nine years later.

The building that bore his name also housed the Attor-ney General, the Secretary of State. Phantom was busted and he knew it.

He had his resignation speech mostly thought out, been thinking on it for a hundred and twenty miles of two lane blacktop. Cocaine coming ashore, two dead, two missing and nobody gave a damn. And he reckoned he already knew the Colonel's response: "Sergeant, that ain't your job!"

The Colonel was at his desk, framed by flags and certif-icates from the Girl Scouts to the Shriners, the Boy Scouts, the National Rifle Association, the National Shooting Sports Foundation, Ducks Unlimited. He got all liquored up once and slapped hell out of his wife and she called the law. They threw him in jail but turned him loose pretty quick. Outside of the original fifty words in the crime blotter and two hundred words the next day in section B, it never really happened.

There is this ongoing curiosity down here called the State Law Enforcement Division, SLED. Black Fords, blue shirts, red ties, satellite phones and machine guns. They were under the direct command of the governor and they played by the rules when the rules were convenient. Then there was the DNR enforcement colonel. He was tough as a heart pine plank when he joined up but desk time took its toll, spider webs of broken veins on nose and earlobes and his neck was creeping over his buttoned-up collar, always too tight. Sheriffs had pull, but there were forty-six of them, one for each county and their sundry jurisdictions stopped at railroads, rivers, highways, wherever the country line played out. They might cross during "hot pursuit," a concept sometimes defeated by slick criminal defense attorneys. But statewide? There was the Director of SLED and the commander of the Highway Patrol, the Colonel was the state's third top cop. If he couldn't fix it, he knew somebody who could.

The Colonel rose to greet him but when Phantom snapped to attention, the Colonel extended his hand. "You are ninety seconds late. Come on, Sergeant, we can't keep the governor waiting."

And finally, it was Phantom's turn to be caught flat-footed, utterly bamboozled.

Sookie Bailey, Republican. Some folks called her Nookie but only Democrats dared and then only very privately. Her parents came from India, her momma wore a red dot and her daddy wore a turban. Then she married Jake and became a Methodist. Jake was a major in the National Guard. When he was deployed to Afghanistan, she could have been vice-president, maybe even president, had such an office been declarable on Fox News. She gave the official Republican response to the Democrat State of the Union Address. She whipped the unions and the Feds to bring Boeing from Seattle to Charleston, Dream Liners and billions. She loved to slip away to creek-side beer joints, steamed shrimp and oysters, but those times were few.

"The governor is very pro-life, you know." Elevator to the first floor, a thirty second briefing. "And oh, we have taken liberty to invite a few friends."

Every year the agency gives out the Bobby Gifford Award for the Officer of the Year. Bobby Gifford was second in command to the Colonel's predecessor and highly esteemed, best known for sorting through his wardens for the best cooks for barbeques, oyster roasts and shrimp boils to impress the politicians he needed to impress. But that was at an awards dinner in January and January had come and gone. A highway patrolman opened the door, the Colonel waved Phantom ahead and the cameras flashed, clicked and whirred.

The governor led the applause. She was a bit angular and she clenched her jaws while she spoke, but otherwise, she was very pretty. She shook his hand and kissed him, once lightly on each cheek.

Her speech was just a blur, something about patriotism, men being men and women being women and bravery beyond the call, all vaguely recognizable and then she said, "In grateful recognition of your contributions and friendship to the State of South Carolina and her people. I do hereby confer unto you the Order of the Palmetto with all the rights and privileges appertaining thereto."

The Order of the Palmetto, South Carolina's highest honor. Another highway cop passed him a plaque, extravagant brass on burl walnut. It took both hands to hold it.

Phantom felt a tug at his britches, Cassie at his side with those spaniel eyes. But she had grown, waist high now. She mouthed the words. "I love you Daddy."

He scanned the crowd. There was Carla, baby at the tit. He caught her eye. She smiled and he smiled back. Phantom had given up on love a long time ago, but he was starting to like this woman and had absolutely no idea why.

And then the governor waved Carla to the podium. The cameras took off again, like cicadas in scrub oaks on a July night when the air gets almost too heavy to breathe. Phantom reckoned Hampy put the Colonel up to the whole shitaree, damn him. The Colonel called the governor and things got complicated real quick. And then Hampy did not show, clear enough a sign, the bastard.

Ain't much call for sergeant wardens with the Order of the Palmetto. Any number of meth-head deer shiners would love to add Phantom Winchester III to their trophy list. The bragging would last about as long as it took the SWAT team to get there. Sheriff Nicky Jacitus hired ex-Marines and had a middling good SWAT team on call pretty quick but it would be too late for Phantom.

Wasn't much time to think. Maybe they were all in on it. Not the governor, no. But maybe the Colonel? And Hampy? Oh Jesus! He didn't know much, but he knew this: There was a million dollars of toot somewhere in those dunes. Two men knew where it was, only one now. And Phantom blew whatever chance he had by delivering this child.

But maybe not.

Carla passed the boy child to the governor and Phantom heard the pop when she pulled it from the tit. Phantom saw the nipple, the governor did too. It was big as a strawberry and almost as red. The child screwed his face, balled his fists and tucked his legs. He almost cried but he did not. The governor tickled the boy's cheek and he gazed up at her face in wide-eyed wonderment. Too bad he was too young to remember it when he grew up.

"I see you are breast feeding him." There was a round of murmurs and giggles.

"Yes ma'am, I make enough milk to feed some third world counties."

"And what did you name him?" the governor asked.

"Phantom Winchester IV," Carla drawled.

ASHES AND FIRE

Early April and they were burning off the plantations again. A fine blue haze lay along the horizon, upon land and sea, and the sky was a grayer shade of blue

Indians burned these woods from time immemorial and the fires popped the seeds of longleaf pine which would not germinate any other way. When DeSoto blundered through the Southeast in 1536, ninety-three million acres of longleaf pine stretched from what would become Virginia to East Texas. But the land was stripped and the strong and rot-proof timbers shipped around the world, from shoring up Bavarian lead mines to framing Buckingham Palace, destroying an entire ecosystem. But there was no such word in those days, no concept of it even. The ivory billed woodpecker, the passenger pigeon and panthers gone, indigo snakes, bears and wild quail nearly so.

But the Longleaf Alliance was fixing to bring it all back and annually fired up ten million acres across the South. Landowner and managers were supposed to hire PhD fire techs and apply for permits and some did. Happy was supposed to follow the smoke and write tickets to those who did not. Violations might be construed as arson, a felony, and if the flames jumped a road or a fire lane and got onto Federal Wildlife Refuge, of which there were many, an Act of Terror, which could land a man in the slammer till he croaked.

Yankees loaded up the 800 lines, asthma and hysteria, the woods were aflame and "Don't worry ma'am, we do this every year" was not a sufficient response. Hampy drove plantation back roads, ate smoke, watched the burns with considerable satisfaction. He chatted up the begrimed crews with their water-packs, shovels and hand-held radios, passed out Cokes and Sprites, but no tickets.

And now he was back in the boat, throttling up from All Joy Landing, a tune running around in his head. "Pay Me My Money Down," a Geechee work song from the Georgia timber docks when they shipped the longleaf overseas.

I thought I heard my captain say, Pay me my money down,
Tomorrow is our sailing day, Pay me my money down.
Oh Pay me, oh Pay me, Pay me my money down,
Pay me now or go to jail, Pay me my money down.

Payback time. But Hampy didn't really know who owed who. Or what either. He missed Phantom but didn't know why. Smoke boiled from the Bull Island woods, a thousand acres aflame. He knew the fire from the smoke it made, white in grass, black in pine straw and deadfall, nothing but a near-invisible washboard crinkling of the air when the flames raced through the scrub palmetto fans. Moonshiners loved palmetto fronds in the old days, fast and hot and scant smoke, green fronds covered the still.

He came ashore at Freeport Marina just as the Yankee day-trippers were heading home. They waited in a chigger bit and forlorn knot at the end of the pier and the sand gnats were eating them alive. Yankees called them no-see-ums, but you can see um if you got good eyes, about as big as a flake of fine ground black pepper. Lord knows how a thing so small can hurt so bad. They get in your ears like skeeters won't. They get up your nose and into your eyes. They get into your hair where skeeters can't. Not clean bites like skeeters. They tear tiny jagged holes and lap blood. Skeeter spray won't kill them and they use bug dope for gravy. Some say sheets of fabric softener tucked in pockets or under the hat keeps them away. It might work, but not good enough.

The island was a National Historic Landmark. In between a couple of failed resorts were nearly fifty Geechee shanties, one room school houses and board-pew churches dating from the late 1800s which drew tourists from Nebraska to Nigeria. Now they were swatting bugs, the Daufuskie Salute. Three hours earlier, they were shoeing flies off their burgers and seafood baskets, the Daufuskie table grace.

Hampy elbowed his way through the throng and his uniform gave him some slack. The boat was fifteen minutes from boarding but still they hovered. Caught on this place after sundown? Oh, hell no! Hampy knew what they knew but they didn't even know half of what he did.

He rented a golf cart from the general store, picked up a map, though he knew damn well where he was going. He gave the pretty blonde at the till his government card. She scanned it and it was good.

Women are the earth and men are on it. Phantom met Hampy in the yard where the sand was loose and ankle deep. His tee shirt was stained with grease and fish blood and his game warden britches were frayed and cut off at the knee. He was packing a Glock as usual and a pair of expensive European binoculars dangled from his neck. There was a Jeep with a spidered windshield, a low front tire and a stove-in fender with a turtle rescue sticker on the door.

Carla came out of the trailer house and stood on the stoop, Phantom Winchester IV on her hip. She looked like a woman from a Walker Evans photo, poor folks during the Great Depression, but Walker Evans took photos in black and white and Carla and the baby were in living color. Her shirt was wet at the nipples from the milk she leaked while the palmettos rattled in the wind, fresh now and off the beach.

Hampy eyed the diapers hanging from the clothesline and wax myrtles thereabouts, fluttering in the sea breeze. "Looks like you done surrendered," he said.

Phantom wanted to slap hell out of him, but he took his hand instead. "And how are you, my brother?"

"Same old shit," Hampy said. "Did you know a shad net had to have two inch mesh?"

"Hell no," Phantom said. "Did you?"

"I do now. They give you your pistol?"

"Give, hell! The bastards charged me for it. One hundred and eighty-seven God-damn dollars," Phantom said. "And thirty-seven God-damn cents."

"Never knew you really liked a Glock."

"I don't. Just used to it, I guess."

"You still looking, aren't you?"

"I still got eyes."

"Seems like you got a dick too."

Carla hollered from the porch, "Supper's ready!"

There was a half bushel of blue crabs steaming on a table made from an empty cable spool upended. A spool makes a fine table for picking crab or butchering fish. Kids can sit on stools and it's tall enough where an adult doesn't have to bend over, easy on the back.

Picking crabs. Most folks got a fingernail under the belly apron, peeled it back, got a thumb nail under the shell and tore it off. Bust off the mouth, pick out guts and lungs and suck up the meat left over. But that's hard for a little girl. "Put them on the table, pull the claws and the legs off and smash 'em!" Cassie's hand came down—smack—and crab-shell splinters flew.

Phantom took the baby. He smiled and gurgled on his knee, old enough now to hold his head up. His head bobbed and daubed like a fishing float when the crappies were on the bite. Carla went to the kitchen and came back with potato salad and pickled shrimp. The potatoes bore a faint trace of curry.

"Always reckoned they'd retire you first," Phantom said.

They were down at the south end, down at Bloody Point, named for any number of savage Indian fights, the first in May 1715 when aggrieved Yamasee went on the warpath and butchered every last white person they could catch. The naval militia caught up with a war party here and left the beach red with blood, twenty-seven Yamasee stretched out upon the sand.

"Me too, but then you went and won that award."

"And you didn't have a damn thing to do with it?"

"No, bub. It was the Colonel's doings."

"And the Governor, too, I suppose?"

"Yep."

"Bullshit."

Sanute brought news of the forthcoming massacre. He was a Yamasee brave in love with Mrs. Frasier, an Indian trader's wife. Sanute came calling one afternoon while Mr. Frasier was not home. He spoke fair English, some Spanish and was greatly troubled. "Bring me agua caliente."

And lo, when hot water was brought to him, he broke out bundles of sacred herbs and infused them in the steam. Then he summoned Mrs. Frasier and when she stood before him, he anointed her head, her brow, her neck and her breasts. "The Creek will be returning the red stick, one moon. You must go and you must go now. Gather no provisions and make no alarm, even now you are being watched. I have left a canoe for you at the water's edge." Then he ran his hand across her beasts one final time, "If you are taken, I promise you this as a final act of my love. Before I let them torture you, I will kill you with my own hands."

"That Indian is crazy," allowed Mr. Frasier.

"Maybe so," Mrs. Frasier said. "But we are going."

They did.

William Bray, another trader, did not. The Indians drove heart pine splinters into his flesh and broiled him alive. It took him three days to die.

"You talk to that Russian girl?" Phantom asked.

"Yep."

"What she say?"

"How you like my poosey, Big Buoy?"

They rode the scarf line the way home, a two-foot cut-bank where the last big tide had sliced into the dunes. There were great corduroy ricks of dead spartina cane, driftwood snags, a couple of rotted off dock piling, pallets with Chinese stencils then suddenly a snatch of black plastic fluttering in the sea wind.

Phantom braked hard, pulled over. Tires gathered sand and the Jeep juttered to a stop. "Son of a bitch, grab that shovel!" Phantom got all itchy around shovels after that day on the landfill.

Hampy dug and the sand flew.

More plastic. "Keep digging," Phantom said.

Hampy worried a hole into the cut-bank, big as a wheel barrow. Nothing but more plastic. He stopped digging, leaned on the shovel, wiped his brow, left grit from the back of his hand on his forehead. Sex on the beach? It was a drink in the Hilton Head bars, when the young Yankee hotties down for spring break flirted with the bartenders, dock monkeys and lifeguards. They just couldn't go back to Ohio or Pennsyl-tucky without it, the drink or the act, and there were ass and heel prints all up and down the dunes and calls to Doctor's Care, the walk-in Doc in the Box, the next morning. "I think I maybe caught something."

"No ma'am, just some minor abrasions. Use this salve.""

"Bub, this plastic is brittle as soda crackers. Been here a

long time. And you call yourself a cop?"

Phantom dropped to his knees and with bare hands, dug like a rabid badger. "It's here somewhere!"

A year ago, Hampy was on his belly not far from this very spot, watching the Flying Cloud, that pretty wood boat out of Thunderbolt, Georgia. What a difference a year makes!

"You ever think they are all in on it?" Phantom mumbled over his shoulder.

Gnats were already starting to gnaw. Hampy twitched, scratched, fretted. "You mean those same bastards who put you up for the award?"

"I don't know what to think anymore." Phantom found a conk shell. It cut a finger but he cast it aside and kept digging.

"What you gonna do if you ever find it?"

"I'm hauling it to God-damn Columbia and throwing it on the God-damn Colonel's God-damn desk, God-damn it!"

"You've lost your freaking mind," Hampy said.

BLOOD MOON RISING

Jeanie loved all living things, the sons of men especially. She trolled the bars on Hilton Head whenever she took a hankering, good picking at the Black Marlin, close to the dock. She slipped one or two over on the last company ferry whenever she could. The next boat was at daybreak, perfect. *Hey baby, I love you, don't miss the boat, holler at you later, goodbye.*

Jeanie had a foot-long alligator in the extra tub and a Great horned owl with a gimpy wing on the porch perched upon a red cedar snag. She named him Hootie and each midnight he came to hand for a piece of raw venison, a chicken breast or a wad of beef burger.

Owl talons would pierce flesh to the bone. So Jeanie had a leather welder's glove with a gauntlet halfway up the sleeve. She bummed it from the boys at the resort mower shop, the boys who kept the golf course in whatever repair they could keep it. She did one of them once. He was just off the clock and she had to shower off the grass clipping afterwards, all itchy where a girl did not need to itch.

She would don the glove and pat her wrist and there would be a sudden rush of wings, like an orgasm on a midnight porch. She'd turn him loose by and by.

Now that he was sufficiently domesticated, Phantom needed a dog, or at least Jeanie thought he did. So she got one, a big Chessie bitch from Beaufort County Animal Control. She bit the mailman and she bit the UPS man and when she bit the FedEx man, three strikes, you're out.

"Hey, Carla, they are fixing to put this dog down."

"That's right, I got a kill order on this dog," the girl at the pound said. "Any problems, there goes my job. Once you walk out the back door with this dog, that's it. I'll tell 'em I killed it and you don't know my name. Get it?"

Got it.

So Jeanie brought the dog to the island and once brought, there was no un-bringing. The dog was the color of a well-done buttermilk biscuit, curly-haired, flop-eared, deep-chested, blockheaded, obstinate, with the most fetching green eyes Phantom had ever seen.

Chessies, officially the Chesapeake Bay Retriever, came off a Spanish ship, a bitch and a sire cast ashore in a hurricane on the Virginia coast. All hands perished but not the dogs.

Subsequent generations exhibited a predictable tenacity.

She came with a name, Buzzy. Perfect. A dog's brain is

hardwired for such a sound. Phantom knew better than try and call a dog Tiberius or Sebastian.

"Hey Phantom, how you like my girlfriend? She like throwing a hotdog down the hall?"

She grinned and wiggled. Phantom ignored her as best as a man could. But Phantom could not ignore the dog, grinning and wiggling too. She was snubbed short to a middling pine with a length of frayed automobile tow strap. She sat at attention, old time shotgun shell calendar perfect and the steady work of her tail cut a clean arc in the pine straw.

"That's a mighty fine looking bear you got there, ma'am."

"She bout pulled my freaking arm off," Jeanie said. "She didn't know where the hell she was going but she was gonna get there first. Jesus Christ. Rub my shoulder please. You want a beer?"

It takes a dog about three weeks to quit missing its last owner and start minding the new one. You got to watch them close meanwhile. Stories make the news from time to time, two, three, five hundred miles to get home.

But not Buzzy. Once she got Lucinda's and Cassie's scent, she was their dog forever. The girls were used to running barefoot, free and wild but still needed some looking after, summertime especially with the snakes and gators on the prowl.

Instead of looking for two kids, Phantom just looked for one dog and he kept a bottle of generic Benadryl handy. Three tabs in raw bacon, repeat as needed, best thing in the world for a snake bit dog.

Hard to know what a dog knows. They can hear and smell a universe humans cannot ever imagine. Maybe Buzzy knew the girls were her last hope. Sure seems like she did. She didn't eat much, table scraps and a couple scoops dry food for breakfast.

Buzzy looked at Cassie with utter adoration and Cassie would tickle her chin, "Buzzy, Buzzy, Buzzy" while Lucinda would smile and chorus, "You fool *gog*."

She slept the first half of every night with one child, the second with the other, didn't matter who came first. Teddy Bear, watch dog, burglar alarm, smoke detector, alarm clock. Carla brushed pecks of beach sand and skeins of dog hair from their beds but it was worth it.

Buzzy moped around the trailer-house while Cassie was at school, grunting and rolling her eyes with considerable drama. But she soon learned the schedule and would lay by the window facing the drive, her chin on the sill, thumping her tail against the floor when she first heard the rattle of the little island school bus. She could hear it long before Carla or Phantom could.

Myrtle Island, Bluffton, on the May River, dark-thirty, Hampy filling out a stolen property report. The DNR seldom bothered with thefts or alleged thefts unless it was a watercraft or watercraft related and this was.

Bluffton was once one single mile square, laid out in the 1820s as a resort town for owners of inland plantations, rife with yellow fever and malaria in those days. The Yankees burnt it in 1863, all but the church which was too beautiful to torch and a couple of houses they forgot. A fishing village on a dead-end road for the next century then it got discovered in the 90s, a nine-fold population increase in ten years, stack-a-shacks, big box stores, Mac-Belcho-Delight fast food restaurants.

Looking to relocate to Bluffton? Can't decide on an apartment complex? Count the bullet holes in the Vinyl siding first.

You'd never know any of this happened, down where the black top ran out, at All Joy landing or on Myrtle Island in the dark, lest the wind was right and you could hear the rumble of traffic on US 278 and the banshee squall of the firetrucks and the wail of the EMT meat wagons.

Hampy had the titles to the boat and motor and he scratched away with a stubby pencil like cops always carry. The citizen held the flashlight.

"I shrimp when the shrimp are running and I pick some oysters for the restaurant trade," the citizen explained, "then I got this little sideline, Commander Zodiac."

Hampy kept scratching. "Commander Zodiac?"

"Yessir. Yankee tourists are crazy about porpoises. I pick them up at All Joy and find 'em a pod of dolphins. When they get tired of that, I land 'em on the beach and lettem pick shells, something to take home, you know."

"When did you notice the boat missing?"

"Late afternoon. I ran up to Circle K to fill up some jerry cans. Bastards stole it while I was gone. Must have been watching."

Hampy tore out the yellow copy and gave it to the citizen along with his business card. "It ain't likely gone far. I'll holler at you when we find it."

"You reckon you'll find it?"

Hampy nodded. "Some drunks joy-riding most likely." And then, almost as an afterthought. "Where you take 'em shelling?"

"Daufuskie," the citizen said. "Nobody hardly goes there. Lots of shells on the beach."

Click.

Midnight. A red half-moon hung low over the west and an ebb tide surf whispered upon the beach, *swoosh, swoosh.* Way out to sea, a drearisome bell buoy gonged on the gentle swell and the beacons in the Savannah channel flashed red, white, green and faithful.

A faint whine of an outboard on the wind, barely audible at first. A two-stroke, a twenty-five, maybe a thirty. A ghost of gray moving on the gray sea and the juttering of a prop chopping bottom. Muffled voices and the green glow of a chemical lightstick, cold light, invisible to infrared. The rattle of an anchor chain and three men splashing ashore. "You stay with the boat," one man said, "and you come with me."

There was a brief flash from a handheld device, GPS. The moon slid down the west and the stars wheeled while the sea sung it's sad, sad song.

"We must move quickly," one man said. "but there is a debt to be paid."

"But you said nothing of debt."

"You will have your money and you will do as I say." Another flash from the handheld. "Only a mile, no more. One hour."

"And when we find them?"

"We will kill them, we will kill them all."

Phantom made the rounds before turning in, an old habit. Nose the wind, eye the moon, listen to the night birds, guess what the tide was doing, piss off the porch. Check the little one, sleeping on his belly, butt in the air. Pat Momma, who mewed in her sleep. Check on the girls. Buzzy sleeping across the foot of Cassie's bed.

Phantom scratched her ears. "How you doing, Yellow Dog?"

Buzzy licked his hand, thumped her tail against the comforter, bump, bump. He turned towards his bed when the dog raised her head, cocked her ears. "Muff?" It was clearly a question. "Muff?"

She looked at the darkened window and in an instant she was no longer a dog, but a dire wolf, a demon. She growled like Phantom had never heard, the low gurgling rumble of a beast from the pit of hell. Phantom killed the lights, palmed his Glock.

"Easy girl, easy. You stay with the kids." Phantom moved to touch her again, but thought better of it.

Hampy came around the north end of the island in the agency boat. The Melrose resort, where the whole shitaree started the year before, the beach club, all lit up but fine now as the loggerhead had all hatched that time of year. There was a green day-marker there atop a sandbar to keep Calibogue traffic in safe water. Slip a hundred yards behind it and there was six feet even at low tide, all the way to Bloody Point, four miles away. Hampy throttled back, ran just hard enough to keep the boat on plane.

Two miles, three and he saw what he knew he would find,

the missing inflatable hanging from the anchor in shallow water. Damn, he was one fine cop.

But now what?

Hampy hit the blue lights, then the floods which lit the boat up like the Second Coming. Scalded by the lumens, the man aboard the Zodiac couldn't tell if Hampy was one man or a dozen. He wanted no fight anyway and put his hands in the air even before Hampy hailed him on the speaker in English and Spanish. The son-of-a-bitch was likely Russian but Hampy couldn't speak it.

Hampy threw him face down in the bilge, put his knee between his shoulder blades, did a quick frisk and got the cuffs around one wrist. He pocketed the man's wallet but there was no time to check his ID.

"They spoke of killing and I want no killing," the man said rapid-fire. "They just asked me to carry something but no killing. You will remember that, won't you sir?"

"I'll mention it to the judge," Hampy said. He grabbed him by the shirt, dragged him astern and got the other cuff around the motor bracket. He pulled out his knife, snick, and there was a hiss and a fine spray of gasoline from the fuel line. "I'll be back."

"Oh please don't leave me sir," he was blubbering now. "The tide she comes now. What if I should drown?"

"You sit still and you'll be all right. Meanwhile, I wouldn't strike no matches if I was you."

There came a distant rattle of gunfire on the wind. One shot, two, three, two more, then too many to count. No casual assassination, Phantom was giving good account of himself.

The first man got it in the guts when he cleared the corner of the trailer, the next two in the chest, bap, bap. He went down with a wheezy thud, the noise a dead buck deer makes when you drop him off a pickup tailgate. First man Phantom ever killed but there was no time to think about that. A slug split the air, a lightning crack just inches from his left ear.

Phantom leapt from the porch, rolled once, came up shooting. But there was nothing to shoot at, just the dark from where the shot had come. Phantom gatored on his belly to a patch of palmetto scrub, good camo, and waited an eternity in four seconds. There was another shot and Phantom unleashed another four as quick as he could, then, click, his Glock was empty.

The trailer door sprung open and Cassie came running, Oh God No! Bullets kicked sand at her feet. Oh Sweet Jesus, save this child!

Cassie belly flopped next to him in the dirt, passed him two double stack Glock magazines, two of the ones he and Hampy had lifted from the goons months before. "You must have dropped these, Daddy. Me and Lucy found them and cleaned them up for you." He slapped one into the magazine well and chambered a round. He tucked her head beneath his right shoulder, shielded her body with his as best he could.

"Hey Copper," a voice called from the dark, "I heard that click. What you gonna do now?"

Hampy was going to kill him first chance he got, but he needed that chance, a half a second, tops. "Take me and let the girl go!"

And then the dumbass walked into full view, pistol in his hand. "I am going to kill her first. And it will be the last thing you ever see, Copper. Then I am going to walk into that trailer and I am going to kill everybody in there, I don't give a good God-damn who it is."

Those were his last words. The window on the trailer blew out and Buzzy launched herself upon him in a mighty snarling leap, jaws open straight to the middle of his chest, a rocket of teeth, eyeballs and fur. The man got off one shot and the bullet hit Buzzy head-on but she rolled him anyway. When the man struggled upright again, Phantom stitched him stem to stern, four, five quick shots to the heart and lungs. Like his partner, he was dead before he hit the ground.

Cassie screamed and crawled to the dog. "Oh no, oh God no, Daddy save her, save her please!"

A dying dog will turn on its owner, shred him in its last breath. Phantom made a snatch at the girl but missed.

But Phantom could do nothing for the dog. She was shot through the heart. Cassie cradled her in her lap as she wept bitter tears. Buzzy snorted, her lips quivered, whickers twitched as she opened her eyes one final time. Thump-thump, her tail upon the sand.

"Oh," Cassie said, "oh!"

And then there was a final welling of blood from the hole in the dog's breast and the light went out of her eyes as her great heart beat one final time.

Cassie set upon the dead man in a fury. "God-damn you, you son-of-a-bitching bastard!" she kicked sand into his open mouth and danced upon his face. Phantom heard the cartilage in his nose pop. One eyeball dangled from its socket by the optic nerve. "God-damn you! God-damn you!" Lord knows how a little girl learned to cuss so.

Phantom took her into his arms and she buried her face in his neck, sobbing. "She died for you, Honey," was the best he could say.

"Momma says Jesus already died for me," Cassie sobbed. "I just want my dog back."

Out on the beach, Hampy listened to the last rattle of gunfire. He got on the cell phone. "Pick up, damn you, pick up!"

Voice mail. Hampy called again.

Phantom answered on the fifth ring. "That you?"

"Oh thank God! You alright?"

"I guess so," Phantom said, his voice shaking. "Call the coroner."

BENEATH SO KIND A SKY

Hurricanes and tropical blows came and went. It was way down in wintertime now but still comfortable in the sunshine if a man kept out of the wind. Jeanie hauled over a hay wagon from the horse barn and dropped it in a sunny spot behind a windbreak of oleander and wax myrtle. She brought over a couple dozen straw bales and sat them here and there for chairs in the trailer house yard. Guests arrived in twos and threes and Cassie and Lucinda flittered among each new arrival, a half-grown yellow Chesapeake dogging their every step, nose and tail working overtime.

Hampy booked the band and Phantom paid for it, Craig Coyne and his rotating crew of sidemen picked up from other bands that might not have a gig that particular night. He called them "Spare Parts."

Craig picked a mean acoustic guitar, every bit as good

as Jerry Garcia and he covered a lot of Grateful Dead tunes. There was a bass player, a man on keyboards and another who grunted away on a digeridoo, the Aborigine instrument from the Outback decorated by a wisp of Spanish moss. They were all good, Nashville good, Muscle Shoals good, too good to be whiling away their lives on Hilton Head. But they had been seduced by the sea wind in the palmettos, the sigh and roll of the sea, the rattle of the halyards against the sailboat masts on the marina docks, the good reefer and the easy picking amongst the Yankee girls. Summer time and the living is easy, the song says and it is summertime here eight months every year. Phantom ran an extension cord out from the trailer-house to run the PA and the amps.

Sam and John Boy were smoking a joint downwind, as this was an official function. Sam was a crabber from Thunderbolt. John Boy was a shrimper from Tybee whose uncle had snagged the Tybee bomb in his shrimp net and drug it six miles and finally hired divers to cut it loose.

The Air Force says it poses no hazard but won't retrieve it because it would be too dangerous. John Boy knows where it is, maybe not exactly but he could get close. He got all lickered up one night and called Hunter Field. "Sir if you are concerned about a bomb, please call the Tybee Island Police."

John Boy knew all about the Tybee Island Police. They busted him for felony flight, after a cop broke his leg in a stump hole running him down.

Sam took a long hit and tried to hold it. He choked and coughed and a whisper of smoke rolled from each nostril. "You know why them cave men drug women by the hair?" he asked.

"Hell no." John Boy took the joint.

"Cause if they drug 'em by their heels, they'd fill up with sand."

A decrepit golf cart rattled, smoked and wallowed up the sand driveway, the Colonel and the Reverend Ben Williams aboard. "In Jesus name, blessings to all who are gathered here!" the reverend boomed.

Craig Coyne did a brief one, two, three on the mike, then struck up his first tune. Ridin' that train, high on cocaine....

The music died when Hampy unplugged the extension cord.

There was a brief flurry of confusion from the band but they were used to playing the creek-side beer joints where a rowdy run on the bass might flip a breaker.

Hampy waved the plug where the band could see it. "Don't play that song."

Craig Coyne nodded and held up his hand. "I understand. Somebody here got a cocaine problem?"

"You might say that," Hampy said.

Ben Williams called the crowd together. Craig Coyne passed him the microphone but he didn't need it. "Jesus says when so ever you gather in My name, I am there among you, even to the uttermost parts of the earth, even until the end of the world."

Carla held the baby on her hip and in her free hand a bouquet of fresh cut camellias, red and white, the only flowers blooming that time of year. Jeanie stood on one side with another bouquet and Phantom on the other. Then came the girls holding hands and their yellow pup, rolling in the sand, pawing and licking at their feet.

"We are gather here to celebrate the marriage of Carla, and...." The reverend paused as he read from his notes, "Phantom?"

"That's right," Carla said, "Phantom."

"Do you, Phantom, take this woman Carla to be your lawfully wedded wife, to have and to hold, forsaking all others from this day forth?"

"I do," Phantom said.

"And do you, Carla....."

"That sounds good to me," Carla interrupted, "let's sign the papers."

And then the band struck up the Jimmy Buffet standard, "Why Don't We Get Drunk and Screw?"

"They say you are a snuff queen, honey, I don't think that's true..."

Hampy was working up a powerful thirst but he dassn't drink as he was in uniform. He dogged Phantom's trail as he circulated amongst the guests, fifty or sixty now. Carla and Jeanie wrestled a great steaming cauldron and dumped five gallons of shrimp, sausage, corn and potatoes atop the spool table, what shrimpers boiled up for lunch on the stern of their boats in the olden days, Frogmore stew, they call it. The crowd gathered round and dug in.

"I almost hope those sons-of-bitches got clean away," Hampy said when he finally caught up with Phantom at the beer keg.

"Who?" Phantom asked.

"Who? You know who! Them bastards we started out looking for."

Phantom worked the tap pump, drew himself a beer. "Hell, I forgot all about them."

"Liar. You never forget nothing."

Phantom shot him his best weasel grin, took a pull on his Solo cup. "You right."

Hampy drew a beer.

"You drinking on the job again?"

"No, I am just going to carry it around to make me feel better."

"Jackass!"

"Oh, I'm fixing to drink it, but I'm going to have a word with the Colonel first."

"Be careful."

"Oh I will," Hampy said.

The Colonel sat alone at a picnic table, peeling shrimp and gnawing at a cob of corn. "Mind if I join you, Colonel?"

The Colonel wiped his lips with the back of his hand. "Might as well, Sergeant, nobody else will."

Hampy slid in on the corner, an old habit in case he had to get up quick.

The Colonel cast his eye across the tattered and bleary assembly. "What kind of company you boys been keeping down here anyway?"

"You're looking at it sir."

"I believe you could drop a net on this whole gang and save the Feds a lot of trouble."

"You don't know the half of it, sir."

"Well, feel free to enlighten, me, Sergeant."

In one clean move, Hampy unsnapped his Glock and

pushed it across the table, butt first. He unbuttoned his badge, slapped it atop the pistol, *whap*.

"You're not quitting on me, are you Sergeant?"

Hampy felt his pulse rise in his ears, booming like hurricane surf. "No sir, I already quit." He took a long pull from his beer. "E pluribus unum."

"What the hell does that mean? You been smoking some of that shit I smelled a while ago?"

Hampy drained the cup. "One among many," he said.

"You better be damn glad you just quit," the Colonel said.

"I am," Hampy said, "and now I am fixing to tell you a story but you got to promise me one thing."

The Colonel pushed his plate aside. "And what might that be, Sergeant?" He paused, "Ex-sergeant."

"That you won't screw it up." Hampy said.

"Oh, I will try not to," the Colonel said with more than a trace of sarcasm.

And at any second the lost bomb might finally short circuit and blow this entire beautiful and troublesome world completely and totally to hell.

But it didn't.

And the band played on, another Grateful Dead tune
Sometimes the light's all shining on me,
Other times I can hardly see

From *The Island Packet*
Feb 11, 2016
A co-owner of a Hilton Head Island adult entertainment club has pleaded guilty to racketeering and money laundering in connection with a Myrtle Beach criminal enterprise.

Michael Rose, an owner of the Gold Club chain with a location on the south end's Dunnagan's Alley, pleaded guilty Jan. 25 to 108 of 132 counts of racketeering, money laundering, conspiracy to commit money laundering and conspiracy to possess with intent to distribute more than five kilograms of cocaine, according to court documents filed in a California federal court.

The Gold Club has had locations in several cities across the country, including in Myrtle Beach, Greensboro, N.C., San Jose, Calif., and Las Vegas.

Business owner Rose is listed as a co-owner of the Hilton Head club with Bill Thomas, according to business license information provided by Faidra Smith, a spokesperson for the town of Hilton Head.

Adult entertainment businesses have operated at 1 Dunnagan's Alley since 1988, though the Gold Club did not open there until 2011, according to town records.

That's the same year Rose and others began working with an undercover agent, who they believed to be a drug lord, to launder $2.3 million through the Gold Club and various Myrtle Beach area nightclubs and restaurants, according to the FBI.

The laundering continued through early 2015.

Rose sought to have the charge dismissed in September, based on "outrageous government conduct" and lack of evidence that he was considering committing a crime before the agent approached and "pressured" him.

"Quite literally, from start to finish, all of the alleged criminal activities were government creations," his lawyer argued.

Judge William Alsup denied Rose's request, and noted that despite any initial reservations of working with the agent,

Rose eventually participated in the criminal enterprise, the Horry News reported.

"Co-defendant Vladimir Handl and Rose depict themselves as innocent and naive saps preyed upon by a government bully," Alsup wrote. "The record, however, shows otherwise."

Still, Alsup also criticized the multi-year investigation, which created the criminal enterprise based on lies, according to MyHorryNews.com.

"One can rightly ask whether the FBI should be out solving real crimes already committed by real criminals rather than encouraging innocents to commit manufactured crimes," Alsup said.

Rose, who is out on bail, is scheduled to be sentenced May 31, along with a second Gold Club co-defendant who pleaded guilty to multiple counts of money laundering on Jan. 5, according to court records.

A third defendant is set to be sentenced in May.

Seven others were charged in the Gold Club case in March 2015, including a former Myrtle Beach police officer and S.C. Highway Patrol trooper who allegedly promised to protect the drug shipments through their law enforcement connections.

The corporate defendant PML Clubs, Inc. — through which Rose operated Gold Club locations and other enterprises — could face a maximum fine of $250,000 for each racketeering-related counts and $500,000 for each count of money laundering, according to the FBI.

Rose faces up to 10 years in prison for each property offense and a maximum 20-year term for conspiracy to possess cocaine with intent to distribute.

Attempts Thursday to reach Rose, Thomas and Rose's attorneys Solomon Wisenberg of Nelson Mullins Riley

Scarborough LLP. in Washington and Daniel McCoy in Myrtle Beach for comment were unsuccessful.

CPSIA information can be obtained
at www.ICGtesting.com
Printed in the USA
BVHW031214180120
569853BV00004B/542